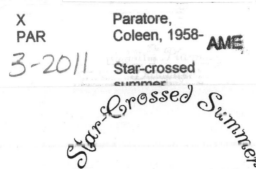

Coleen Murtagh Paratore is the author of several books that have been published in the US. She lives in Albany, New York, with her husband and three sons. She is a hopeless romantic and lifelong believer in the magic of Cape Cod.

D0168567

Also by Coleen Murtagh Paratore

The Wedding Planner's Daughter

The Wedding Planner's Daughter: Playing Cupid
'Funny and sweet – you'll love it' *Mizz*

And coming soon
The Wedding Planner's Daughter: From the Heart

The Wedding Planner's Daughter

Star-Crossed Summer

Coleen Murtagh Paratore

MACMILLAN CHILDREN'S BOOKS

First published in the USA 2008 by Simon and Schuster Books for Young Readers
First published in the UK 2008 by Macmillan Children's Books

This edition published 2009 by Macmillan Children's Books
a division of Macmillan Publishers Limited
20 New Wharf Road, London N1 9RR
Basingstoke and Oxford
Associated companies throughout the world
www.panmacmillan.com

ISBN 978-0-330-45009-6

1 3 5 7 9 8 6 4 2

A CIP catalogue record for this book is available from
the British Library.

Printed and bound in the UK by CPI Mackays, Chatham ME5 8TD

To my beautiful sister,
Noreen Mahoney,
with my deepest admiration.

I love you, Neen.
– Col

Contents

When life throws you a pit, plant a cherry tree.
— Willa Havisham

Lucky Days

We'll begin at dawn.

– Thornton Wilder, *Our Town*

When I see the sun rise out of the sea, sometimes I think I will burst with thanks for a world so lovely as this. There is such hope in that moment, such possibility.

Before the sun comes, I sit alone on the cliff, staring at the rainbow ribbons out where the water meets the sky, and I wait with the wind and waves, the gulls and fish, the morning star, even the moon sometimes, we're all together *waiting, waiting,* until, at some silent moment, the horizon hatches before our eyes and a diamond bird of light bursts upwards, wet and shining from its sea-mother nest.

Promise me you will watch the sunrise at least once in your life.

It is a miracle. Godgrand.

If I miss the sunrise, but I am still the first to arrive on the beach, those are lucky days too. I sink my foot in the sand like a flag, an explorer claiming new land. I survey the scene before me and smile. *Mine, all mine.*

This morning I walk out on to the Spit, a narrow peninsula, about a mile long, the Atlantic all around. Bay on one side, ocean on the other. Today I start on the bay path, the calmer, peaceful side. The wind blows soft against my cheeks, the waves lap gentle as a lamb. On the other side, on some days, the surf soars and wind roars mighty as a lion. And all that separates the lamb and the lion is this little strip of land.

Just sand really. Grains of sand. Millions and millions of them.

Alone, each is barely visible. Together, they make a beach.

Once upon a time, the Spit was so big there were hotels along it. Hurricanes and northeasters have taken their toll. So has the pounding of countless feet, beachcombers like me. Each year the Spit gets skinnier. It could wash away any time now. One good storm might do it. It's important that its backbone, the sand-dune, stays strong.

The sand-dune runs spine-like down the centre of the Spit. When I was little, the dune was a mountain, thrilling and forbidden. Up, up, up I would plod, stand panting victoriously proud on top, then run slip-slide-giggling down.

Now the mountain is a hill. I can see across it in places.

Frosting the dune is a field of seagrass, long flowing green hair. Small birds, grey and white plovers and terns, for some reason choose to nest here. Then, once they do, those silly little birds imagine they are bigger than they are. They fight bravely to fend off heavy-pawed dragons running free from their owner's leashes and the aerial assaults of seagull monsters searching for breakfast eggs.

Yesterday was warm for April. It is much cooler this morning. Feathers of fog flit past me like fairies. I swipe them away and laugh.

When I was little and first came to Cape Cod, summers to visit Nana, fog used to scare me. Fog wasn't weather at all. Fog was a ghost that would swallow me up if I didn't hurry home and hide. Now fog seems ethereal, romantic.

I reach for the silver heart, the locket Joseph Francis Kennelly, 'JFK,' gave me on Valentine's Day. He looked so handsome that night, brown hair skimming the collar of his tuxedo, blue eyes glittering in the firelight. I thought I might faint. I kept telling myself, *Breathe, Willa, breathe*.

He knew I was disappointed when I opened the locket and it was empty. Two halves of a heart, no pictures. The dimple on his cheek deepened as he smiled. 'The *girl* decides who to put in it. But . . . I hope you decide it's me.'

'Oh, it's you,' I said and I kissed him. I kissed him first. Then we danced in the barn, just the two of us, the most perfect night of my life.

When I reach the tip of the Spit and turn, I can almost feel the ocean current shift. I am on the lion side now. Wind fills my ears and whips my hair back. I close my eyes and breathe it in.

Everything seems more alive here. Louder, faster, saltier. Two seagulls are trying to out-squawk each other, battling for the same poor scuttling crab. No fishermen this morning, not a single boat. Maybe a storm was forecast.

On clear days as I walk I look for beach glass and orange and yellow jingle shells. Sometimes I find buoys, lures, castle buckets. Last week an emerald earring, just one.

The fog is getting thicker now. It wets my face like rain. I pick up my pace. I'm late anyway. I'm on breakfast duty at the Inn.

My family owns the Bramblebriar Inn, just outside the centre of town. I hope Rosie is making blueberry pancakes, warm maple syrup, sausages on the side . . . *wait* . . . There's something ahead there on the jetty, out on the final rock. I walk forwards, the fog growing thicker. It's hard to see anything clearly.

As I get closer, I can see it's not a fisherman, because there's no pole. How odd to be just standing there out on the edge of a jetty on a morning like this. How curious.

I walk closer. The figure turns. It is a girl,

about my age. She looks familiar, but I'm not sure. 'Hi,' I shout over the wind. The girl stares at me. She cranes her head forward, side to side, looking, as if she too is trying to see if she knows me.

I reach the jetty and nearly slip as I step up on to the first boulder. The fog is thickening like pudding. The girl is motioning to come closer, or maybe just waving. I guess we do know each other. 'Hi,' I say again, louder. I hop over to the next boulder, then the next, careful not to slip. Wouldn't want to fall in on a day like this, not able to spot jagged rocks and coral, not to mention the eels. I hop across to another flat spot.

Just then, there's a break in the fog. I can see her face. Dark eyes and skin, long curly black hair. She is beautiful. The girl smiles as if we know each other. I have never seen her before. The wind is picking up, waves crashing in louder, must be nearly high tide. These last several boulders will be covered with water soon. It won't be safe to stand. 'Hi,' I say again.

The girl nods and then turns back towards the sea. She spreads her arms wide like a heron before flight, then raises them above her gracefully and dives.

What? It's too early in the season to swim. Even for the bravest, Cape water won't be warm for months. I leap on to the next rock, then the next, and when I reach the last I look down. I don't see her anywhere.

I stand there looking, looking. She has to come up for air. I call to the foaming water. 'Hey. Are you all right?' Did she swim left or right or straight out? I search and search. It starts to rain. Shivering, I zip my jacket, pull up the hood. I keep scanning the water. 'Hello. Are you OK?' Where is she? Why hasn't she surfaced? My heart is pounding. What if she hurt herself? What if she . . .

I head back fast along the slippery rocks, and when I reach the beach I start running, eyes glued to the water as I do. Where did she go? Why doesn't she come up for air? I'm definitely late now. Mother will be mad. I run towards the beach steps. My bike is at the top. I'll phone for help at the nearest cottage. As I run I stare, eyes burning, fixed on the water, searching, searching. Where is she?

And then all of a sudden the girl's head pops up. She looks towards the shore like a carefree harbour seal. I run to the edge of the water and scream, 'Are you OK?'

'Yes,' she shouts, treading water, wiping hair away from her eyes.

'Are you *sure* you're OK?' I ask.

'Yes,' the girl shouts, sounding annoyed. '*Are you?*'

2

Talk About Surprises

Anything serious goin' on in the world since Wednesday?

— **Thornton Wilder,** *Our Town*

Am I? Am I OK? Unbelievable. I'm fuming as I ride home cold in the rain. Here I was worried about *her*, trying to help *her*, and she acted mad at *me*! Who is that girl anyway? And she was on my beach, *my beach*.

It isn't until I turn the corner on to my street, see the old stone fence and the Bramble Board message:

Spring forward toward your dreams.

that I feel myself calming down. A girl couldn't

ask for a nicer home than the Bramblebriar Inn.

Happy yellow daffodils, and cheery pink and purple tulips line the winding driveway. I park my bike, head up the porch step. *Hmmmm*, breakfast smells delicious.

When my mother married Sam Gracemore last year, we renovated his grandmother's old estate and opened the Bramblebriar Inn. People in town said we uncovered a treasure. Mom gave up her wedding-planning business and Sam gave up teaching to run the place. I help in the kitchen and take care of the library, the games room and the Bramble Board.

The Bramblebriar Inn is elegant, but warm and cosy too. When our guests come back to visit us again and again, we welcome them home like family.

The main house is three storeys high, white with green shutters, four tall brick chimneys, and a widow's walk on the back rooftop. On a clear day you can see Nantucket Sound. There are thirty rooms in the main house and several smaller buildings on the property, a renovated barn big enough for dances and parties, acres of grass, trees and flowers, a huge round garden labyrinth and a pond where you can swim in the summer and ice-skate in the winter.

'Sorry I'm late, Rosie. Be right there.' I flip my wet sandals off by the door and race up to change. My stepfather, Sam, is the main chef at the Inn, but we've just hired Rosie to handle breakfast and desserts. My freshman English teacher, Dr Swaminathan, went to India on family business, and Sam is substituting for him this semester. I'll miss Dr Swammy, but I'm happy to have Sam back as my teacher again. That's how I first met Sam. He was my seventh-grade English teacher. From the moment I met Sam I knew he would be the perfect husband for my mother, the perfect father for me. I spent months playing Cupid, trying to get them together, and finally it worked.

I still call Sam 'Sam', but I am planning on calling him 'Dad' on Father's Day. I think that's the best gift I could give him. It's been a long time since anyone called Sam 'Dad'. Sam was married before, long ago, but his wife and son were killed in a car crash. His little boy was only two.

When I come down to the kitchen, Rosie is dicing vegetables with the flair of a celebrity chef on television. She puts me to work squeezing oranges for juice.

Rosie can't be more than twenty. She has a baby named Liliana. Nana told me that Rosie's husband ran off after the baby was born and never came back. Nana heard about the situation and helped Rosie get the job here.

I think it must be so sad for Rosie having her husband abandon her like that, and so hard having to leave her baby to come here, but Rosie doesn't bring her troubles to work. She's friendly to me, Mom and Sam, but she keeps her private life private.

'How was your walk, Willa,' Rosie asks.

'OK,' I say. I'll wait and tell my friend Tina about that annoying girl in the water. 'What are you making, Rosie? It smells wonderful.'

'Frittatas, home fries, cranberry-nut muffins.'

'Hmmm, can't wait.'

'Morning, ladies,' Sam says, coming into the kitchen. 'Willa, your mom said another magazine called yesterday. You won't let all this fame go to your head, will you?' Sam winks at me and smiles.

'No way, Sam.' I guess I should tell you I'm something of a celebrity here in Bramble. People say I saved the Bramble Library, which I guess is true. Last September I was elected Community Service Leader for the freshman class at Bramble Academy, and we had to find a way to make a difference. My friend Sulamina Mum, she's a minister, said to pick a cause I care about. Well, I heard that the Bramble Library was being shut down. They were going to send all our books, *Bramble books*, over to the Falmouth Library. I was so mad I couldn't see straight. That's another thing you should know about me. I love books. I mean I love, love, love, love, *love* books. And that was my library, *my library*. No way would I let them close it.

The freshman class put on dance parties here in the barn and then a fancy Valentine's prom to raise money, but it still wasn't enough. It looked like the library was lost until, lo and behold, our favourite Inn guests, the Blazers, of the Blazer Buick fortune, came through with big bucks, and to cut a long story short, the Bramble Library lives.

Mom comes in freshly showered after her morning run. She grabs a bottle of water from the fridge, whispers something to Sam, and he says, 'Sure, Stella, OK.'

'Willa,' Mom says, 'can we talk to you for a minute?'

Rosie looks uncomfortable, like maybe she should leave, but she can't. The guests will be expecting breakfast at eight.

'Why don't we go into the library,' Sam says.

This sounds serious. Oh no, what now? Is everything all right with Nana? Is everything all right with the Inn? They aren't thinking of selling it are they?

Mom and Sam sit next to each other on the couch. He wraps his arm around her and says something I can't hear.

'We have some news,' Mom says. 'I know this

may come as a bit of a surprise to you, Willa . . .
but Sam and I . . . are going to have a baby.'

What? My stomach somersaults.

Mom smiles at Sam. He nods at her. The tide
is changing in my brain.

Sam looks at me, tilts his head to the side,
squinting his eyes like he's trying to read my
thoughts, like he's wondering if I'm OK with this.

Talk about surprises. It was always just me
and Mom. Now me, Mom and Sam. I've been an
only child for fourteen years. I'm a freshman in
high school for goodness sake . . . *and now I'm
going to get a little brother or . . .*

'Willa,' Mom says, walking towards me, 'are
you OK?'

I burst into tears. I hug her. 'I'm so happy for
you, Mom. And Sam.'

When I hug Sam, he keeps his hands locked
on my shoulders and stares into my eyes like he's
trying to read them. Sam knows that 'happy' isn't
the only way I'm feeling right now. 'Willa—' Sam
starts, but I shake my head 'no'. I don't want to
spoil my mother's joy. 'I'm good, Sam. I'm late for
Tina.'

Now I *really* need to talk to my best friend.

3

Maybe She's a Mermaid

I've got to tell you something, because if I don't . . .
I'll burst.

– Thornton Wilder, *Our Town*

When I get to the Belles' house, Tina is up in her room sprawled out on her bed, studying the new Hotties catalogue.

'Hey, Willa, perfect timing. Which bikini do you like better, this one or this one?'

I look at the bathing suits. 'They're pretty. Why don't you get both?'

'Oh good, Willa, thanks, you're right.' Tina breathes a sigh of relief. 'I was feeling a little guilty because I already ordered three yesterday and I'm reaching my card max for the month, and Daddy's threatening to cut me off again, but, hey, you can never have too many bikinis, right?'

'Right,' I say, sticking my chest forwards, picturing the boring navy blue one-piece in my drawer from last year. I look at the models in the Hotties catalogue. It would take a miracle between now and beach season for me to look like a 'hottie' in one of those bikinis. Maybe I should do more push-ups or eat more broccoli or something.

'Here, Willa,' Tina hands me the catalogue, 'take it. We get a bunch of these a month. Mom and I are gold-club customers. Maybe you'll see something you like. And don't be afraid to show off your shape. You have such a cute little shape.'

The word 'cute' grates on my ears. I'm sick of being 'cute'. Nobody calls Tina 'cute'. People call Tina 'gorgeous'. She has a face like a movie star and long, silky blonde-white hair like the angel wig I wore in the kindergarten Christmas pageant.

'Tina, wait till you hear this. I have really big news. Mom and Sam are expecting a baby.'

'A little sister?' Tina claps her hands all excited. 'Ooooooooh, how *cute*!' She bops up and down on the bed. 'A little sister? Oooh, I can't wait. Tell Stella I'll babysit any time, all the time, for free. Oh, Willa, we'll have such fun shopping for her, dressing her up, taking her out to lunch –' Tina leans forward, her big brown eyes sparkling – '. . . just think about all those tiny baby dresses, shoes, pocketbooks . . . oh my gosh, we've got to get her tiny baby ears pierced . . . and take her to the spa for her first little mani-pedi . . . in pink, of course . . .'

'Whoa, Tina, wait. She's not even born yet. And what if it's a boy?'

Hmmmmm. Tina's face darkens. 'Well, that would rule out the mini mani-pedis . . .' Then she quickly lights up again. 'But baby-boy clothes are fun too! Aunt Amber loves buying stuff for her nephew. Little farmer jeans and baseball caps . . .' Tina stands up. 'Anyway, I'm not worried,' she says, flipping her hair back, case closed. 'I know it will be a girl.'

Tina looks at me. 'But what about the big sister? Are you OK with this?'

Exactly. 'It's a big shock. I couldn't believe it at first. I had no idea they wanted a baby. I mean they're sort of old for it aren't they? And I'm in high school. I mean, it would have been nice to have somebody to play with when I was little, but—'

'Oh, Willa, come on. It will be so much fun.'

'I guess you're right. I'm starting to like the idea a bit . . .'

Tina claps her hands. 'Good. Now, can I be her godmother? I want to be the first to know when she's born. OK? The first.'

'Well, I can promise you fourth, maybe. Mom . . . Sam . . . me . . . then you. Deal?'

'Deal.'

We get a bowl of chips and some soda. I tell Tina about this morning on the Spit. About the strange girl on the edge of the jetty who dived off into the fog. 'And I thought she'd drowned. I was all worried, shouting to her, running to call the police and then all of a sudden she surfaces like a seal and asks if *I'm OK*.'

'Wow,' Tina says, 'and you didn't recognize her?'

'No. At first I thought she looked familiar, but, no, I've never seen her before.'

'That's weird,' Tina says. 'Who goes swimming alone that early in the morning? In April? On Cape Cod? Jamaica, maybe, Cancun, maybe, but Cape Cod, no way. That water's freezing. She must be an Eskimo.'

'I don't think she's from around here.'

'Well, it's way too early for tourists,' Tina says, 'and it's not a holiday weekend . . . wait, Willa, hold everything –' Tina's mouth drops and her eyes go bug wide – 'Maybe she's a mermaid.'

'Tina,' I crack up laughing. 'This isn't a movie.'

'No, really, she could be.'

'Yeah, right. Listen, you mentioned your Aunt Amber earlier. How's her business doing?' Tina's Aunt Amber owns a matchmaking company called The Perfect Ten. Aunt Amber says the secret to love is finding the person you have ten important things in common with: similar views on religion, politics, having a family . . .

That gave Tina the idea to make up a compatibility questionnaire for our Valentine's dance. Questions like What's your favourite ice cream, sport, pizza topping . . . Tina insisted that everybody had to answer the questions. Normally the boys would have bolted, but we had a hook. One of them would win a date with my friend Suzanna Jubilee Blazer, the Southern belle beauty-pageant-winning daughter of the Blazer Buick family I mentioned before.

Tina sent the completed questionnaires to Aunt Amber, who fed the information into her computer. The matching couples were announced at the dance. I never got to go to the dance after all the work of planning it, because I broke my foot during a yodelling accident that morning. It's a long story. Anyway, it all turned out perfectly in the end. JFK left the dance early and came to the Inn. He threw a stone up at my bedroom window to get my attention.

When I saw him standing there so beautiful in his tux, I nearly fainted. I changed into my pink gown, spritzed on some perfume and hobbled down the stairs. We danced in the barn and he gave me the locket. It was the most romantic night of my life. Now we are officially a couple. We talk every day, go out to dinner and the movies . . .

But as I'm remembering that night he gave me the locket, I start getting angry again. Ruby Sivler has that effect on me. You see, just when JFK gave me the locket and I was laughing and crying I was so happy, he said 'Guess who my match was for that compatible couple thing?' I said, 'I don't know, who?' all the while screaming hopefully, '*Me*, I'm hoping, *me*,' inside.

'It was you,' JFK said, '. . . and another girl too.'

Ruby Sivler. I was sure of it. Ruby's been after Joseph since seventh grade. I just knew she'd find a way to fudge the answers so she'd appear to be his perfect match. I started fuming inside, thinking how I'd get back at Ruby for cheating, when all of a sudden JFK said, 'But the eleventh question broke the tie.' JFK and I were the real perfect match after all. Of course. And before I knew it I kissed him. I kissed him. I kissed him *first*. And we slow-danced while Cupid fluttered above us up in the rafters . . .

'Willa?' Tina says. 'Earth to Willa.'

'Sorry. I was thinking about how Ruby fudged the compatibility test so she could get matched with Joseph at the dance. When is she going to stop being such a sneaky . . . ?'

Tina has a weird look on her face. The look she gets when she's hiding something. 'So,' Tina says, picking up the Hotties catalogue. 'What else should I order?'

'Tina?'

'What?'

'You're hiding something.'

'No I'm not.'

'Yes you are.'

'No.'

'Yes.'

'No.'

'Tina stop it. Tell me. What?'

Tina's face scrunches up like, 'Are you sure you want to know?'

My heart is pounding. This can't be good. 'Tell me, Tina, what?'

'OK.' Tina sits back down on the bed. 'Now don't start getting all worried. I worry about you worrying so much. But Ruby wasn't the other person JFK nearly got matched with. There was this girl at the Valentine's Dance—'

'Who? What girl?'

'I don't know,' Tina says. 'She was wearing this glittery eye-mask, you know, like they do at a costume ball, and everybody was wondering who she was. Then Dr Swammy, oh he looked handsome in his white tuxedo—'

'Stick to the story, Tina.'

'OK, sorry. So Swammy announced the Compatibly Cupid Dance and started naming the couples. He called out me and Jessie. Oh I wish you could have seen how hot Jessie looked . . . OK, sorry, and then Swammy called "Joseph Kennelly and Willa Havisham" and then "Joseph Kennelly and Mariel . . ." somebody or other.'

'Everybody was like "Mariel who?" Some guy shouted, "Way to go, Joe, two for one." And then the girl with the mask and the green gown edged her way forward and stood right next to Joseph. "Is that Willa?" Jessie asked me. And I'm like, "Duh, no, Willa's at home with a broken foot." And then I reminded Dr Swammy about the tiebreaker and he said, "Thank you, Tina," and he consulted the eleventh question tiebreaker list and announced, "Joseph Kennelly and Willa Havisham." And the girl in the mask turned and walked out of the room without saying a word. In fact, I don't think I heard her say a word all night. It was really strange—'

'Tina, why didn't you tell me?' I feel like I'm underwater.

'Oh, Willa, you were so happy about the locket and kissing JFK and your private little prom in the barn that I didn't want to spoil it for you. I knew you'd start worrying. You worry way too much, honey, and there's no reason to. Joey Kennelly is obviously crazy about you—'

'Describe her to me, Tina. This Mariel.'

'Well, you couldn't really see her face because of the mask. But her skin was dark and beautiful and she had this amazing black ringlety hair . . .'

4

My Town

Very ordinary town, if you ask me . . .
But our young people here seem to like it well enough.

— Thornton Wilder, *Our Town*

My stomach is a tide pool swirling. *Why can't anything stay perfect for two seconds?* On the way home from Tina's, I stop at Mum's. I always feel better when I talk to Mum.

Sulamina Mum is the minister of Bramble United Community 'a home for every heart'. You don't have to be any certain religion to belong. Mum says we're all connected back to the very same one and only God and that the only prayer we need is two words: 'thank you'.

I love Mum. She's like another mother to me. Except she's my friend.

'Hello, Willa,' Mum calls, happy to see me. She's sweeping her porch steps. 'How's it going?'

'OK.'

Mum stops sweeping and looks at me, hard. She lowers herself down on the top step and pats the spot next to her. 'Sit and spill, little sister, sit and spill.'

I tell Mum about the masked mystery girl, 'Mariel', and how she was a perfect match for JFK at the Dream dance and how I have this awful suspicion that she was the girl I saw swimming in the fog this morning and what does that all mean . . . and on top of that, all of a sudden after fourteen years my mother has decided to have a baby and how embarrassing since I'm a freshman in high school and . . .

Mum listens without saying a word. I love that about Mum. She's the best listener I know. When I finish, she takes a deep breath and lets it out slow. '*Hmmmph*. I agree. That sure is a lot to hold in your heart.'

'Well, what should I do?'

Mum takes another deep breath and lets it out more slowly than the last.

'The way I see it, Willa, nothing much you can do about either situation.'

We sit there quiet for a minute. The wind chimes tinkle softly. A bee buzzes by.

'So what's your new cause going to be,' Mum says.

'My *new* cause?'

'For Community Service. You're still the leader, right?'

'Right.'

'And you're done saving the library, right?'

'Right.' I see where this conversation is heading.

'And it's only, what, the start of April, and you've got nearly three months left of school . . . *hmmmph* . . .' Mum raises her eyebrows, shrugs her shoulders, and then stares off straight ahead.

I never knew a person who could say so much without saying a single word.

'OK, OK. I get it.' I laugh. 'We should find another good cause, another way to make a difference, right?' I stand up and shake my head. 'Anybody ever told you you'd make a good

♡ ♡ ♡ **28** ♡ ♡ ♡

spiritual director, Mum, like say a minister or something?'

'Seems to me I've been told that once or twice in my lifetime.'

Mum's front door opens and cane first, foot second, Riley Truth steps out. Riley is Mum's long-lost high-school sweetheart. They just reconnected at Christmas. I sort of played Cupid, since I was the one who kept encouraging Mum to try to track him down. And she did. And he came. And they've been happy as honey ever since. I just hope they won't move back down South. I'd be so sad if Mum left Bramble. It would be like the sun leaving the . . .

'Join us for a walk, Willa?' Riley says. 'I promised this pretty lady the first ice-cream cone of the season. Although it's sure stone colder up here than home, isn't it Sully?'

Mum laughs and holds out her hand. Riley helps her up. Mum wraps her big black pillowy arms around Riley and kisses him on the cheek. 'Don't worry, old man,' she says. 'I'll keep you warm.' Riley laughs and winks at me.

I giggle. 'I'll leave you lovebirds to it.'

There's still some time before dinner, so I head to Sweet Bramble Books. It's the book and candy shop my grandmother owns, my favourite place in Bramble. Give me a good book and a bag of candy and I'm a happy camper.

The sun has long since burned away the fog. Smiley-faced pansies, purple, red and yellow, nod at me from the window boxes along Main Street. Bramble is one of Cape Cod's original sea-port villages. We still have some cobblestone streets. Most of the buildings are brick or white with clapboard shutters, some have plaques that read, 'National Register of Historic Places'. Bramble United Community, we call it BUC, stands tall at one end of Main Street. Bramble Free Library, all covered with ivy, waves back from the other end. In between are clothing shops and restaurants, a two-screen movie theatre, some tacky tourist shops, the Town Green where we have concerts in the summer, Fancy's Fish Market, Earl's Hardware, the new Sea Spa where Tina and Ruby get their beauty treatments, two art galleries, Wickstrom's jewellers, where JFK bought my heart locket, the post office, the bank, Hairs to You, where my hairdresser, Jo, designed my new one-side-curly, one-side-straight hair, Miller's Pharmacy, Cohen's Card shop, Delilah's florist, Bloomin' Jean's ice-cream parlour, a two-for-one T-shirt store, and . . . *ahhhhh* . . . Sweet Bramble Books.

The bells on the door jingle as I open it. Scamp runs happy to greet me. 'Good dog,' I say, giving him a hug. Scamp licks my face. Nana looks up from the candy counter.

'Willa, good, you're just in time. Come have a chocolate-covered strawberry. The berries aren't in season yet, but my produce supplier gave me a crate this morning.'

I bite into the warm milk-chocolate jacket. 'Delicious, Nana.' Sweet strawberry juice dribbles down my chin.

'Remember when you used to love chocolate-covered cherries,' Nana says. 'You always told me to leave the pits in the centre for good luck.'

'Then I ate so many I got sick of them.'

Nana laughs. 'That's OK. Tastes change. Now you're my chief saltwater-taffy tester.'

Cape Cod is famous for its saltwater taffy, in every flavour you could wish for.

Over on the book side of the store Muffles miaows and leaps down from her sunny window perch. When Gramp Tweed was alive, every Friday he would leave a new book for me on that window ledge. Muffles would sit on it until I came.

It was just this past December that Gramp died of a heart attack. We all miss him like crazy, Nana especially. She still has some really bad days. Though she is never one to feel sorry for herself, never wants us to worry about her. But I do. Nana has had heart trouble of her own. I keep reminding her to take a walk every day.

Muffles miaows, rubs her grey coat against my leg, circles around me, and miaows again. I pick her up and scratch under her neck the way Gramp did. I rub my nose against her tiny wet nose. I bet Muffles misses Gramp too.

'Did you hear Mom and Sam's news?' I ask.

'About the baby?' Nana says, looking at me over the bridge of her glasses.

I nod.

'Yes. Stella called me this morning.' Nana doesn't sound pleased. She shakes her head and sighs. 'That daughter of mine never ceases to surprise me. What is she thinking of? A baby at her age?'

'But, Nana, Mom only just turned forty. Lots of women have—'

'I know, I know, but the older you are, the greater the risks of something going wrong and—'

'Nothing will go wrong,' I say. 'My mother is the healthiest person I know. She's strictly vegetarian now and she jogs five—'

'Jogs blogs,' Nana says. 'Stella better slow down. And forget the vegetables. She better start eating some good American Angus beef or she won't be getting enough protein. And how is she going to run an Inn and take care of an infant and . . .'

I walk away so Nana can rant and rave in peace. Let's just say Nana and Mom don't always see the world through the same pair of sunglasses.

There's a new display of books on the main

table. *Our Town* by Thornton Wilder. I pick up a copy and read the back jacket.

'*Our Town* was first produced and published in 1938 to wide acclaim. This Pulitzer Prize-winning drama of life in the small village of Grover's Corners, an allegorical representation of all life, has become a classic.'

Sounds good.

'*You are holding in your hands a great American play. Possibly* the *great American play . . .*' Donald Margulies.

'*. . . touches the soul like a miracle.*' Albert Einstein.

The Albert Einstein? Wow.

I grab two more chocolate-covered straw-berries and plop down on the old tweed couch. Gramp and I used to sit here and 'book talk' every Friday afternoon after school. I open *Our Town* to Act One.

'This play is called "Our Town" . . .'

A long while later I'm still reading. There are chocolate smudges on the pages. I don't want to put it down.

'You should try out,' Nana says.

'Try what out?'

'The play. *Our Town*. Upper Cape Repertory is holding auditions, next week I think it is. My friend Gail George dropped off those fliers on the counter. That's why I ordered in the books.'

'Mmmmm, maybe. Can I keep this copy?'

'Of course. Any book you ever want. Gramp always said you were his best customer.'

I give Nana a hug. She smells like lavender. 'Are you doing OK, Nana?'

'Fine as I can, honey. Day by day.'

'You're getting out for your walks, right? And you're taking your heart medication, right?'

'Willa, you are such a worry wart,' Nana, shakes her head, laughing, pushing me towards the door. 'Go home now, but come back this weekend, I need you to rate some new taffies for me. Summer's coming and I've got to be ready.'

I take a yellow flier off the counter and stick it inside *Our Town*. I fill a bag with my current favourite flavours of saltwater taffy: lemon-lime, chocolate and peppermint.

'Thanks for the book, Nana, and the candy.' I hug her again.

'Any time, honey. Any time.'

Our guests are having cocktails and hors d'oeuvres on the front porch when I get home. I grab a small plate of cheese and crackers and a handful of grapes and sneak up to my room. I finish reading *Our Town*. I know who I want to play.

Emily. She's the star of the show. She loves her town the way I love Bramble. Everyone is so kind and good to one another. Emily is the smartest girl in her school and she's in love with a boy named George Gibbs. She tells him, 'All I want is someone to love me.' And he says, 'I will, Emily.' And she says, 'And I mean forever. Do you hear me? For ever and ever.' And then the next scene is their wedding day.

It's just so perfectly romantic. I want that part. I am perfect for that part.

Now, if only JFK will audition for George . . .

5

Entire Towns of Butterflies

*Is there no one in town aware of social injustice
and . . . inequality?*
*Oh, yes, everybody is . . . Seems like they spend most
of their time talking about who's rich and who's poor.*

– Thornton Wilder, *Our Town*

'April break is turning into a nightmare,' Ruby
Sivler complains to me and Tina at lunch on
Monday. 'An absolute nightmare.'

'You're going to Mexico, right?' Tina says,
looking all concerned.

'No-o,' Ruby says. 'Well . . . yes . . . we *were*.
Mommy booked us four deluxe beach-front
suites at the brand-new Grand Highness Royale
in Cancun. She booked them last July. *Last July*.
That's how long ago she booked them . . .'

Four beach-front suites. It's just Ruby and her

sister, her mom and dad. They each need their own suite?

'And then some storm hit last month and ruined the entire beach. All the cute little striped cabanas, the palm trees . . . I guess the waves washed right up and ruined all three pools and the hot tubs too. Can you imagine?'

'Hurricane Igor,' I say, 'it was awful. Lots of people lost their—'

'Well, anyway,' Ruby says, cutting me off. 'Thankfully our travel agent has connections and she was able to book us back to Grand Cayman Island. We were just there last year, so it'll be *boring,* but at least I'll get my spring tan.'

'Thank goodness for that,' I say.

Tina looks at me and rolls her eyes.

Tina's right. Ruby is harmless. It's just that she also seems to be totally clueless about the real world. People lost their houses, their businesses, some lost their *lives* in that hurricane, and all Ruby can think about is how it inconvenienced her *vacation*?

I can tell Tina sympathizes with Ruby. They have a lot in common. They used to be best friends before I moved to Bramble. Tina's rich too. Her family always goes some place tropical every holiday break, winter break, spring break . . . My family is 'middle class'. Although Sam says we're rich by world standards. He's always cutting out articles in the paper about countries where children have to beg for food or where mothers have to walk for days with babies strapped on their backs just to fill jugs with clean water . . . It's like Mum was trying to tell me. The job is never done. There is always another way to help make the world a better—

Tina elbows me hard. 'Look,' she whispers.

JFK is heading towards our table.

'Come on, Ruby,' Tina says, standing, trying to block Ruby's view of JFK. 'Let's get dessert. They've got fudge fancies today.'

'Ooh, yummy,' Ruby says.

I don't even have time to worry about my hair or anything before JFK sits down across from me. 'Hey,' he says and smiles.

'Hi, Joseph.'

Why do I still feel like entire towns of butter-flies are hatching in my stomach every time I see him? We're a couple now. When does it get less scary?

'Do you want to do something Saturday,' he says.

'Sure.'

'Like what?'

Anything. Anything. Dinner, a movie, watching the clock tick . . .

'I don't care, whatever. How about you?'

'Maybe we could hit the beach for a while, grab a pizza at Zoe's after?'

Butterflies be gone. I take a leap. 'How about if I make us a picnic? It's supposed to be warm all week.'

JFK smiles. My left hand holds my right hand down to resist touching that dimple. And those eyes, those eyes. Could they be any bluer?

'Sure, but I invited you,' he says. 'What do you want me to bring?'

Yourself. Those peppermint lips . . . 'How about dessert?'

He laughs. 'I don't know. That might be out of my league.'

'A frisbee maybe?'

'Frisbees I can do. I'll bike to your house around two. Good?'

'Good.'

Oh yes, very good. Very, very good.

After dinner I look for Sam. He's in his study on the third floor. It's a small yellow room, lined with books from floor to ceiling, with a narrow stairway leading up to the widow's walk. Years ago wives would pace back and forth up there hoping to spot their husband's ship. The seafaring life was harsh though, and many men never made it home.

The door is ajar. Sam is at his desk writing furiously fast. Catching fireflies, I bet. That's what we call those moments of inspiration when words are coming fast and free in our heads, and we have to catch them *quick, quick*, like lightning bugs in a mayonnaise jar, before they fly away.

I stand patiently in the hall, waiting. I'm curious to know what Sam is writing, but I won't interrupt a moment like this. When Sam first showed me and Mom this room on their first official date, he said he was working on a book. He hasn't mentioned it since. I peek back in again, then again.

When Sam finally stops writing, I knock.

'Willa, hi, come in.' Sam closes the notebook and slides it into the top drawer. He doesn't want to tell me what he's working on. 'What's up?'

I tell Sam how I'm searching for a new cause for our class. Saving the Bramble Library was good, but now it's time to move on. And where to begin? So many bad, sad things in the world. So many people to help . . .

'Willa,' Sam says, eyes shining. 'I'm proud to be your . . . *in your* family.'

I know he was going to say 'proud to be your father'. Just wait until June, Sam.

'It really doesn't matter what you choose,' he says. 'I imagine you are going to do many important things in your life. This is just the next way you'll make the world a little better. We are so lucky here in America, not all Americans, but us, our family, we are healthy, fed, educated. We are lucky even to have the luxury of looking around to wonder how we can share a bit of the goodness we've been given.'

'But freshman class meeting is Friday and I'd like to have a proposal.'

'Anything you do will be more than has been done before.'

'I don't want to ask people for any more money—'

'Forget about money,' Sam says. 'Money is a band aid. People connecting with people is where the real good stuff happens. Person to person. Teaching someone how to read. Helping someone find a job . . .'

'But, Sam, where do you begin?'

'Inside. Listen to your own voice, Willa. I always find that if I shut up long enough and listen, the answer comes.'

I am dying to ask Sam what he's writing, but I respect that if he wanted to tell me, he would. 'Thanks, Sam, goodnight.'

'Night, Willa, sweet dreams.'

'Oh, wait, Sam, what are we reading next in class?'

'Follow the yellow brick road.'

'*The Wizard of Oz*?' I laugh. 'Isn't Oz a little

young for high school? We've been studying Shakespeare all year with Dr Swaminathan.'

'And that's wonderful. But I don't know when I'll get another chance to teach literature again, so I thought I'd do some personal favourites.'

'But Dorothy and Toto, Sam? What's to study? Everybody knows the story.'

'Actually, many people only know the movie version. The original book by L. Frank Baum is brilliant in its simplicity. I think it is the finest, uniquely American fairy tale. The quintessential journey theme, searching for the thing we think we want most, trying to find a way back home . . .'

That night I write in my journal. 'On 18 June, for the first time ever, I will say, "Happy Father's Day, Dad."'

Dad, Dad, Dad.

Sam will be so happy.

6

The Mystery Girl

Oh, earth, you're too wonderful for anybody to realize you.

– Thornton Wilder, *Our Town*

I love *Our Town*. I love Emily. I have to get the part.

There I am on the stage, a hush falls over the theatre, the audience dabbing tears, leaning forward to catch each beautiful word:

Good-by, Good-by, world. Good-by, Grover's Corners . . . Mama and Papa.

Good-by to clocks ticking . . . and Mama's sunflowers. And food and coffee.

And new-ironed dresses and hot baths . . . and sleeping and waking up . . .

*

I already have half the lines memorized.

'You're trying out for a play?' Tina asks, all excited. 'Oh, can I come too?'

For as long as I've known Tina, it's been her dream to be a soap star. I didn't think she was interested in the theatre. 'Do you even know the story?' I ask.

'No, but I'll read it tonight. How hard can it be? When are auditions?'

'Next week.' My heart is pounding. I don't want Tina to try out. Nana's friend Gail George said the director wants to cast the entire play with young teenage actors. Tina might not get all the subtle nuances of the play, but she's gorgeous and dramatic. What if she wins the director's heart with her charm?

I want to be Emily.

'The stage is different from television, Tina. In the theatre you are right there, a stone's throw from the audience, so close you can reach out and touch them. You have to be totally into character. It's all about the story. It's the truest interpretation of the writer's actual—'

'Well, excuse me, Willa.' Tina crosses her arms in front of her chest and flips her angel hair back, case closed. 'Don't get your big book brain all bent out of shape. You don't think I can do it, do you?'

'I didn't say that.'

'Don't you remember, Willa, after we wowed them at that town-council meeting, Doctor Swammy said we gave a brilliant performance. He said we should both try out for the spring—'

'This isn't some cheesy Bramble Academy production, Tina. This is *Upper Cape Repertory* . . .'

Tina giggles.

'What?'

'Upper Cape Repertory. Sounds like a contagious disease.' Tina puts a fist under her chin like a microphone and makes her voice deeper. 'Attention, ladies and gentlemen, we interrupt our usual broadcast with a special report . . . stock up on tissues and nasal spray, we have a serious *upper cape repertory problem* on our hands—'

'Cut it out, Tina.'

Sometimes I wonder how we are best friends. We are so different.

When I stop by the Bramble Library to tell Mrs Saperstone I'm auditioning for the role of Emily Webb in *Our Town*, her face gets gushy like she's going to cry.

'*Our Town*. I love that play. You would be the perfect Emily, Willa. Or, the Stage Manager. I actually think the Stage—'

'No. I want to be Emily.'

And on our date Saturday, maybe I can talk JFK into auditioning for George Gibbs. Emily Webb and George Gibbs get married in the play . . .

'Well, either part, Willa, really any role would be wonderful. I think it's probably my favourite play ever . . . Oh, wait, lest I forget. I've got two books for you.'

Now that Gramp is gone, I rely on Mrs Saperstone – and Sam, of course for recommendations. Life is getting busier and busier with school and soccer and helping at the Inn. I don't want to waste time on so-so stories. I want to read the best books. Gramp always said to read the good ones while you're young, because you may not have time when you're older. I'm beginning to see what Gramp meant.

Mrs Saperstone hands me two books. 'Quite a talented pair, those Brontë sisters. Emily wrote *Wuthering Heights* and Charlotte wrote *Jane Eyre*. They were both published right around the same time if I'm not mistaken . . .'

As Mrs Saperstone talks, I move to look out the window. The forsythia bush is in bloom, and daffodils, tulips, grape hyacinths. Something moves behind the whale spoutin' fountain. I have a feeling as if someone is watching me. I move to the far corner of the window and wait, one eye peeking out from the curtain folds. Sure enough, I see something move again. Then I see her face, the girl from the beach. 'Mrs Saperstone, come quick. Do you know that girl?'

When Mrs Saperstone reaches the window, the girl is gone.

'She's about this tall,' I say, 'really pretty, dark skin, long black curly hair . . .'

Mrs Saperstone's face lights up with a smile. 'That sounds like Mariel Sanchez. She's new in

Bramble. You two should meet, Willa. You'd like her.'

I feel a cold stab of jealousy. *No. I don't like her and I don't want you to either.*

'Isn't Mariel such a pretty name,' Mrs Saperstone says. 'She says it means sea-bright. Isn't that lovely? Sea-bright.'

Sea-bright my butt. Sea-hag, maybe, sea-monster . . .

'Mariel's in here all the time,' Mrs Saperstone babbles on. 'I'm pretty sure she's home-schooled. She comes in every afternoon around one o'clock. And what a voracious reader. She gobbles up books like us, Willa. And she's not afraid to tackle the tough ones. You two would have a lot to talk about.'

'You've got that right,' I mumble.

'So you already know each other?'

'No, not really.'

'Well, I'd be happy to introduce you when—'

'No, that's OK, Mrs S. Thanks for the books.'

'Sure. Good luck with the tryouts, Willa. Keep me posted.'

I turn to leave.

'You know what,' Mrs Saperstone says, 'I just remembered. Mariel is reading *Our Town* too.'

'Well, isn't she special.'

Mrs Saperstone looks surprised.

'I'm sorry. That's cool. It's a good book.'

First my beach. Then my boyfriend. Now my books too.

Who is this strange girl anyway?

7

The Other Side of Bramble

Everybody has a right to their own troubles.

— **Thornton Wilder,** *Our Town*

Outside the library I quickly scan up and down Main Street. There, two blocks up, I spot her. Head down, I start to follow.

Mariel Sanchez is far enough in front that if she doesn't turn round she won't notice me. Just in case, I pull the hood up on my slicker and put my sunglasses on.

Mariel is walking slowly, like she's in no hurry at all. I follow her out of the centre of Bramble, past the public elementary school, the high school, the gas station. My heart is pounding. My hands are sweaty. I feel like a spy.

Mariel keeps walking, further and further. I look at my watch. I'm late for home. Mariel turns. She's heading towards the water.

I should go home right now, but I'm curious. I've gone this far, it's hard to stop. I want to see where she lives.

Mariel turns on to one of the nicest streets in Bramble. Wow, does she live here? Big old sea-captain houses with wrap-around porches and rolling green lawns where clans of families congregate in the summer, and fancy cars lining the driveways.

But no, Mariel keeps walking. And I keep following.

Mariel walks with her head straight ahead, not turning to notice things. She doesn't even seem to acknowledge the people she passes by. How rude. A few seconds later when I face those same people, I say 'hello'. We are very friendly here in Bramble.

Mariel struts by the legendary lilacs in front of the Captain Greenwall Inn, gorgeous thick purple bunches hanging down like grapes in a vineyard. She passes by like she doesn't even see them. I could never resist smelling those lilacs. Mariel resists. Then a few steps ahead, she stops and comes back, plucks off a few branches and continues on her way.

When I reach the Captain Greenwall, I stick my whole face in the sweet soft purple and breathe it in. Down on the pavement I see the tiny buds that fell when that strange girl broke off her bouquet in haste.

Mariel turns on to Surf Drive. For a few moments I can't see her. I walk faster to catch up. When I get to the corner, I spot her. She is walking quicker now. I pick up my pace too. Past a supermarket, a pizza place. There aren't any houses on this strip. I follow her for what feels like another mile. Past the cemetery, a boarded-up building . . .

We are on the other side of town now. It's amazing that this too is Bramble. Like the lamb and lion side of the Spit. Connected, but so far apart.

There's an awful stench in the air. I see a sign for a 'refuse recycling plant'.

Mariel takes another turn and I follow. Past

an ugly apartment building, then a trailer park. I really should go back, but I've come this far . . .

Then all of a sudden Mariel stops. She opens a mailbox, peers in, closes it. She moves on and I follow until I am standing in front of the sign for the Oceanview Inn: 'Tourists Welcome'

I know this place. It's not an inn at all. There is no view of the ocean. No view of anything nice. The Oceanview is a dumpy, rundown motel. Tourists have long since stopped coming here. Paint peeling, shingles falling down, windows grey with dirt. Diapers and blue work shirts hang from a clothes line between two trees. A solitary swing dangles at an odd angle, one chain longer than the other. A rusted metal slide lies tipped over in the mud beside it.

Mariel knocks on a door and enters. Moments later she comes out with two small dark-haired children, one clung to each hip. She goes to the next door, sets the children down, fumbles with a key, and then they go in. I count down the number of doors, number six.

I can't believe she lives here. I helped Nana deliver food here last Thanksgiving morning.

Poor people rent rooms by the month. It's just a step up from a homeless shelter, Nana said.

We brought turkey, mashed potatoes, and all the fixings. I counted five children in one room. I couldn't believe a whole family was living in that one crummy room.

'People can't afford apartments, let alone houses on the Cape any more, Willa. It's a big problem. There are all these low-paid workers, mostly doing jobs that support the tourist industry: cleaners, cooks, cashiers, gardeners . . . But people can't support families on minimum-wage salaries, let alone ever buy a house or put their kids through college.'

I should go. I know I should leave, but I am strangely curious to find out more about this girl. I inch my way down along the rooms, one, two, three, four, five, my heart pounding. I reach the window. The drapes are open.

This is wrong, an invasion of privacy. Just one quick peek. I know I shouldn't. I have no right. Just do it. Look quick.

The room is dark. Mariel is on the floor, kneeling, hands folded, head bowed in front of a dresser. There is a statue on the dresser, a candle flickering, a photograph of a woman with black curly hair, a glass filled with lilacs. The dark-haired children are standing up in a playpen, watching Mariel intently with huge brown eyes. Two neatly made single beds, a lamp and a stack of books on the nightstand, a small refrigerator with a microwave on top. I hear Mariel mumbling, like she's praying. I turn away, ashamed.

A large red van pulls up. 'U are the U in UCADS' is written in bold letters across the side, 'Upper Cape Association for Disabled Citizens' underneath. The van stops and a lady comes around and slides open the door. 'Mr Sanchez,' she calls. Sanchez, that's Mariel's last name. The lady presses a button and a ramp slides out, making a *beep-beep-beeping* sound as it descends to the pavement.

When the ramp clunks down, a dark-skinned man in a wheelchair appears at the top of the ramp. He looks about Sam's age. I see the strong muscles on his forearms as he wheels himself down the ramp. 'Thanks, JC,' he says, 'see you tomorrow.'

I turn quick to avoid him, but the man spots me. For a moment we just look at each other. His eyes are deep brown pools. They are the saddest eyes I've ever seen.

I turn and hurry home.

8

Ding-Dong Ding-a-Ling Happy

*People are meant to go through life two by two. 'Tain't
natural to be lonesome.*

— **Thornton Wilder,** *Our Town*

'Willa, come up here,' Mom shouts when I get
home. She's in one of the small guest bedrooms.
Maybe she's thinking about converting it into a
nursery for the baby.

'Guess who's getting married,' she says, all
excited.

'Who?'

'Guess. You'll never guess.'

'I don't know, Mom, who?' And then I picture
Sulamina Mum. Riley and Mum. I'd be so happy
for them, but what if they decide to move back
South . . .

'Give up?'

'Yes.'

'Suzanna Blazer! She just got engaged and she wants to have the wedding here!'

I start to laugh. 'That's wonderful!'

Suzanna Jubilee Blazer, we call her Suzy-Jube, is the gorgeous daughter of our best and nicest customers, Chickles and Bellford T. Blazer. A date with Suzy-Jube was the prize that lured all the boys in Bramble to our Valentine's dance. She was just crowned Miss American Role Model. 'That's great, Mom. Who is she marrying?'

'His name is Simon Finch and he's a drummer in a band – country music I think. I forget the name. Suzy met him on her Miss Daisydew tour last year. Chickles says Simon "doesn't have two nickels to tape together for a dime", which I guess means he's not rich, but the Blazers don't care. They're millionaires. All they care about is that Suzy is happy. Chickles said she's never seen two people so much in love. They are, I think she said, "ding-dong ding-a-ling happy" and they want to tie the knot as soon as possible.

They've booked the entire Inn for the second Saturday in June, the tenth. The rehearsal dinner will be the night before, of course. I'm going to have to rebook the reservations we already have for that weekend but . . .'

'This June? Two months from now? Why the hurry?'

'Simon's band is going on tour . . .'

'Well, good for them. I'm happy for them.'

'Me too,' Mom says. She walks over to the window and looks out. 'I was actually thinking lately that it might be time to start hosting more weddings here at the Inn.' She turns and looks at me with an odd expression on her face and then turns back to the window. 'The labyrinth and gardens are so beautiful, and now that the barn is all renovated, with the right lighting and flowers it could make a quaint chapel, and we could do something with fountains on the lake and white tents on the lawn for the reception. I know it's a lot to take on with a new baby on the way and—'

My heart beats harder. 'Mom?'

She turns and smiles at me. She knows what I'm going to say.

'Can I please help you plan Suzanna's wedding?'

'Yes. I would love that, Willa.' She walks over and touches my arm. 'I know we got off to a rough start the first time. But we're both older and wiser now and—'

'Partners?' I say.

'Partners,' she says.

I hug her tight and the tears come. Happy tears for both of us.

After dinner I finish my homework and call Tina.

'Wait until you hear this. We're back in the wedding-planning business. And this time Mom and I are going to be partners.'

'Whoopee!' Tina says. 'That's great. Now, Willa –' her voice gets more serious – 'this is important, so listen. You better get online right now and start researching. Keeping track of what's "in" and "out" for weddings is like keeping track of shoe styles. If you miss a week, you're dead. The last thing you want to do is plan some old-fashioned . . .'

Tina dreams of the day she'll say 'I do'. She already has an album filled with pictures of wedding gowns and bridesmaids dresses, destination wedding packages . . .

'You'll need a signature cocktail of course,' Tina says.

'A what?'

Tina sighs. 'Oh, Willa, please. Don't you read the celebrity magazines? Anybody who's anybody has a fancy drink – a signature cocktail – created especially for their wedding.'

'What about champagne . . .'

Tina sighs louder. 'Willa, please, champagne is *soooo* last season.'

Later I open my journal and start to write. So many good things are happening at once. JFK . . . *Our Town* . . . a baby on the way . . . and now Suzanna's wedding!

I've been keeping a chronicle of my life since September of eighth grade, when I inadvertently caused my wedding-planner mother's most famous wedding, the two soap stars from *Forever Young*, to end in disaster. I was actually trying to do something good for the bride and groom, but my best intentions backfired into a colossal nightmare that made headlines nationwide and resulted in Mom deciding to give up Weddings by Havisham and move us to Maine to live.

The day we left Bramble was the saddest day of my life, but my wonderful friend Mr Tweed – this was before he married Nana and became Gramp Tweed – gave me a journal. It had a brown cover with a sunflower on the front. I poured out all my anger and sadness into that blank book, and every time I wrote I felt better.

When we moved back to Bramble, I bought myself a new journal and then another and another. They are lined in chronological order on the top shelf of my bookcase, right there with my 'Willa's Pix', my very favourite books in the world. I don't write every day, but I do try to catch the highlights. It's amazing how life can change so quickly, like the wind, like the weather. One minute everything is happy and sunny, then it's foggy or raining so hard you can't see a foot ahead.

I can't believe we are getting back into the wedding-planning business. *How fun.* All those years when my mother ran 'Weddings by Havisham' she pushed away every man who might want to marry her, and she locked me out of her wedding-planning world. I guess she worried that if I got too wrapped up in dreamy fairy-tale wedding stuff that I would spend less time on school. It has always been important to her that I get good grades and set my sights on college. I was actually forbidden from going into her studio, but I had a key and would sneak down at night to see the easels which displayed the twelve perfect ingredients of whatever master-piece wedding she was working on at the time, quietly adding my own thirteenth secret ingredient . . .

Now, Mom is happily married to Sam and they are going to have a baby and we live in a gorgeous Inn and I have a wonderful father and one of my favourite people in the world is getting married and I am going to help plan her wedding!

I open *Our Town* and stand in front of the mirror. I stare at the girl looking back at me. Curly hair on one side, horsetail straight on the other; blue eyes, my one and only really good feature; skinny body, like a ten-year-old. I turn to Act One. Emily is talking to her mother.

Emily:	Mama, will you answer me a question, serious?
Mrs Webb:	Seriously, dear – not serious.
Emily:	Seriously . . . Mama, am I good-looking?
Mrs Webb:	Yes of course you are. All my children have got good features; I'd be ashamed if they hadn't.
Emily:	Oh, Mama, that's not what I mean. What I mean is: am I pretty?
Mrs Webb:	I've already told you, yes . . . I've never heard of such foolishness.
Emily:	Oh, Mama, you never tell us the truth about anything.

I finish all the lines from Act One, then move on to Act Two. Auditions are a week from Saturday. I just *have* to get this part. I just *have* to be Emily.

I pull out the bag of taffy from my nightstand, open up a peppermint one and pop it in. *Hmmm, good.* Which book tonight? *Wuthering Heights* or *The Wizard of Oz*?

I pick the yellow brick road.

9

Come Home Cape Cod

I'm going to make speeches all my life.

— Thornton Wilder, Our Town

By Thursday afternoon, I still haven't come up with a good idea for our next Community Service Project and freshman class meeting is tomorrow.

'How about a race for the heart association,' Mom suggests. 'Maybe in Gramp's memory.' My mother runs 5k and 10k road races to raise money for various charities.

Mrs Saperstone has another thought. 'Maybe your class could become literacy volunteers,' she says. 'It only takes a few weeks to learn how to teach someone to read. It would be a perfect follow-up to your campaign to save the library. We do the training right here and a new session is starting soon.'

'How about a book drive,' Sam suggests. 'A lot of schools lost everything in that hurricane down South last month,' Sam says. 'Maybe you could collect books to restock a school library? That would be a fine contribution.'

On Friday morning I'm in the kitchen making tea when I see Rosie's pay cheque on the counter next to her purse. I shouldn't look; it's none of my business. But I do.

What? That's all Rosie makes for a whole week working here? That's less than Tina spends on clothes in a week.

I go and find my mother. 'Why don't we pay Rosie more?'

Mom raises her eyebrows. 'How do you know what we pay Rosie?'

I tell her how I snooped, but that isn't the point.

'It's none of your business, Willa,' Mom says, 'but that's actually several dollars above the minimum wage. Rosie doesn't have a college degree and—'

'Why does that matter? She's an awesome cook, especially desserts. She should have her own bakery or something. So what if she doesn't have a degree? How is she supposed to take care of Liliana and buy a house for them and put her through college some day—'

'Whoa, Willa. A house?' My mother lowers her voice, looks around to make sure no guests are nearby. 'Rosie's lucky she can afford an apartment. She's lucky she has this job—'

'You mean Liliana is never going to have her own house? A yard with a swing set and—'

'Willa.' Mom smiles. 'You have such a good heart. It's wonderful you care so much, but . . . hmmm, wait, you made me think of something. I was just reading in the paper about a new organization called Come Home Cape Cod. Yesterday's paper, I think. They want to raise money to build houses for low-income Cape Cod families—'

That's it. 'That's great, Mom, thanks!'

I go to up to my room to do some research. I

find the article about Come Home Cape Cod in the *Cape Cod Times*. JFK's father is the publisher. Maybe he knows more about it. The story talks about how finding affordable housing has become a serious problem on Cape Cod. Developers are swallowing up land and building expensive vacation homes while many people who grew up here are being forced to move off Cape because they can't afford to live here.

Come Home Cape Cod hopes to build ten homes a year. It says it costs about $50,000 to build one of these houses, but if they can get land donated and contributions of materials from building companies and free labour from roofers and electricians and other services, that it can cost less.

I find information on the numbers of Cape Codders who are living in poverty and about what the average Cape Cod worker makes and how many people are living in temporary shelters, places like the crummy Oceanview Inn . . .

This is going to be great.

*

When I share my idea at freshman class meeting though, let's just say I don't get a standing ovation.

'Oh, Willa,' Ruby Sivler says, 'give it a rest, will you? We did the Library. Isn't that enough? It's almost summer. Time to think about pool parties and beach parties and boat trips to Nantucket and the Vineyard and . . . well . . . I don't want to feel all sad and guilty about poor people. I mean, my mother and father give money, they are like the biggest contributors to the Cape Cod Symphony and . . .'

I look over at the boys. Jessie has his headset on. Luke's playing a video game. JFK smiles at me. He shrugs his shoulders. 'I think it's a great idea,' he says, 'but fifty thousand dollars is a lot of money—'

'It doesn't all have to be in cash,' I say. 'We can get businesses to contribute, someone to give us the land, a lumber company to supply the wood.'

Tina scrunches her nose, then sighs loudly. 'I know you mean well, sweetie, but I agree with Ruby. It just sounds like an awful lot of . . .

work . . . to me. Nobody's making us do this, right? I mean we all did our twenty-five hours with the library thing, right?'

Every student at Bramble Academy is required to do twenty-five hours of community service during each of our four years of high school. 'Well, yes, technically we've all met this year's obligation, but—'

'Willa,' Tina says, tilting her head at me like come on, let it go. 'We're all really busy . . .'

I look around at my classmates, Emily, Gus, Trish, Shefali . . . Nobody else seems interested either. 'Well, what about a 5k race for the heart association,' I say.

'Too much work, Willa,' Ruby says.

'How about being literacy volunteers. It only takes two weeks to train—'

'Too much time, Willa,' Tina says.

'Well then,' I say, 'what about collecting books to send to a school that lost its library in the hurricane . . .'

'You mean in Cancun?' Ruby perks up.

'No,' I say, 'in America.'

'Now that sounds just right,' Tina says. 'I've

got books in the basement I'd be happy to throw . . . I mean . . . *give* away for a good cause.'

The bell rings. 'OK, everybody,' I say. 'Show of hands. Who's in?'

Everybody raises their hands. Tina pulls Jessie's hand off of his headset and holds it up in the air. He smiles at her. They are so in love.

Unanimous. 'OK, then, books it is. Let's start collecting today. I'll get permission to store them in the old gym. Try to get as many good children's books as you can find. Ask your relatives, your neighbours. The more the better . . .'

But I'm not done with Come Home Cape Cod.

When I get home I write an editorial letter and email it to the *Cape Cod Times*. I say that I'm a high-school student here on the Cape, a wash-ashore who feels like I was born here, I love this place and the people who live here, how I think it is wrong that some people who were born and raised here can't afford apartments, let alone a house, and that I just found out about the Come Home Cape Cod organization and that I hope anyone who can possibly contribute money or materials will do so. Give as much as they can, as soon as possible. I list the address and telephone number. *Thank you.*

Now I feel a little better.

After dinner I tell Sam what happened at the meeting. 'You're a natural born leader, Willa. I'm proud of you. Maybe you'll be mayor or senator or *president* some day.'

I laugh. 'I thought you hated politicians, Sam.'

'No, I'm just disappointed in the lack of vision in our country. There used to be leaders we could look up to and respect. People who inspired us. John F. Kennedy, Martin Luther King . . .'

'You mean democrats, right, Sam?' Mother and Sam are always arguing about politics. Sam is a Democrat. Mom's a Republican.

'I mean leaders, Willa – humanitarians who motivate people to look around and care about others. It was good that you wrote that letter. You never know who your words might inspire.'

Later, when my homework is finished, I check through my book of famous quotations and head down to change the Bramble Board. President J. F. Kennedy loved Cape Cod. His family had a home here in Hyannis and he walked the Cape beaches for inspiration. He was a big believer in community service. In one of his most famous speeches he called on every American to join in and do their part:

Ask not what your country can do for you; ask what you can do for your country.

I stand back and read President Kennedy's words on the Bramble Board. Two new guests, the Carlsons from Connecticut, are coming up the driveway. They stop and read the quote. They smile and nod at me.

Back up in my room, I finish practising Act Three of *Our Town*. '*I can choose a birthday at least, can't I? – I choose my twelfth birthday. Oh, I want the whole day.*'

I look out of my window, up at the sky. The North Star, the Big and Little Dippers . . . I wish I could see a shooting star. I can't believe that in all the years I've searched the sky, I have never seen a falling star. I imagine it must be very lucky.

After I write in my journal, I prop up my pillows, open my bag of taffy, wrap my quilt around me like a cape, and set out on to the foggy, whimsical, windswept moors of *Wuthering Heights*.

Heathcliff is so romantic.

10

Beach Date

Try and remember what it was like to have been very young. And particularly the days when you were first in love; when you were like a person sleepwalking, and you didn't quite see the street you were in, and didn't quite hear everything that was said to you . . .

– Thornton Wilder, *Our Town*

Saturday is warm and sunny – perfect for my beach date with JFK.

I find my favourite shorts from last summer. Good thing they still fit perfectly. Unfortunately so does my favourite yellow T-shirt. When am I ever going to get a chest? I change into a white tank top with a blue chambray shirt over it knotted in the front, slide on my red sneakers, comb the straight side of my hair and puff up the curly side, put on sunblock, mascara, my cherry-flavoured lipgloss and then my locket.

I open the heart and look at the upside-down faces. Our school photos. Me on one side, JFK on the other. I close the heart and polish it shiny. Hopefully I can convince Joseph to try out for *Our Town*. How romantic would that be? Me in a wedding dress, him in a tux, waiting for me at the altar . . .

Rosie is leaving for the day, but she stays to help me with the picnic.

'Are you sure you don't mind,' I ask.

'Not at all,' Rosie says. 'I hear your boy is quite a catch. I'd like to meet—'

'Oh, sure, Rosie, but not today, OK? This is our first official just-the-two-of-us date. Before we've just met at Zoe's or something with Tina and Jessie. Today will be the parents' interrogation day and I don't want him to get too embarrassed.'

'No problem, Willa,' Rosie says. 'Next time.'

We wrap up thick pieces of barbecue baked chicken, a container of pasta salad, Cape Cod potato chips, peaches, rolls, soda, plates, forks and knives. A wicker basket would be more romantic, but an insulated beach bag is more practical. 'Get some sugar cookies,' Rosie says. 'I just stocked the jar. They're probably still warm.'

Every afternoon, from two till four is teatime at Bramblebriar. We keep a big blue jar filled with cookies for our guests to enjoy with tea and coffee. Every day has a fresh new batch . . . chocolate chip, oatmeal raisin, Heath-bar crunch . . .

There are several guests hovering around the table. I make small talk and budge to the front as tactfully as I can. I do live here after all.

Rosie hands me some pink cloth napkins. 'Fancier then paper,' she says.

'Thanks so much, Rosie.'

'You're welcome, Willa. Have fun!'

The doorbell rings right at two o'clock. Mom and Sam are waiting in the vestibule.

'Mom,' I say, nervous, catching a quick look in the hallway mirror. 'Please just say hello and let us go, OK?'

She opens the door. 'Hi, Joseph, come in.'

JFK looks like he should be on the cover of *Cape Cod Life* magazine. Cut-off denim shorts hung low on his hips, white pocket T-shirt, sandy brown hair tucked behind his ear, a frisbee under his arm. He looks tanned, like he's been out sailing all day.

An alarm bell wakes the towns of butterflies in my stomach and they all start batting their wings at once. He is so beautiful.

'Hi, Willa.' JFK cocks his head, shy. He turns the frisbee around in his hand like he's steering it for support.

'Hi, Joseph.' I set down the picnic bag. 'I think you know my mother, Stella Havisham.'

JFK shakes her hand. 'Ms Havisham, it's a pleasure.'

'Nice to meet you formally, Joseph.'

'And I know you know my stepfather, Sam Gracemore.'

'Mr Gracemore,' JFK shakes Sam's hand. 'Started *Oz* last night. It's good.'

'Glad you liked it, Joe,' Sam says, smiling.

I pick up the picnic. 'All set?'

'What time will you be home,' Mom asks.

'Is nine OK?' JFK says.

'That's fine,' Mom says.

And then, thank all the angels in heaven, we're off.

JFK hooks the picnic bag on to the handlebars of his bike. I put a beach blanket and the frisbee in the basket on mine. 'Ready?' he says.

'Ready.' And off we go to Sandy Beach.

The bike lane is narrow. JFK goes ahead of me. I follow along behind him, the sun on my face, wind whistling in my ears. I feel so happy and pretty and lucky. I picture us holding hands walking out on the Spit, eating dinner, kissing . . .Then before I know it we are pulling into the parking lot, setting our bikes in the rack. I don't remember one street we passed. It's like I dreamed myself here.

There are several people on the beach. It's warm. We walk down the steps and kick off our sneakers.

'Where should we put this,' JFK says, holding up the bag.

'Let's walk out a bit,' I say. *I'd like to walk all the way out to that secluded little scallop of beach,*

*our special spot, where you kissed me on the cheek in
seventh grade . . .*

'Good, let's go,' he says, slinging the picnic
bag on his shoulder.

I walk next to him. He lets me have the level
ground by the water. The ocean is calm; there's a
light feathery breeze. The sky is the colour I used
to pick from the crayon box to paint the perfect
picture when I was little.

We arc around a young boy and his mother
building a sandcastle. It's quite an elaborate
affair, moat and everything. The boy unloads a
cement-mixer pail of sand, complete with sound
effects. His trusty assistant packs it smooth. Past
them are some little girls. They hunker together
and giggle as we go by. Further out, a couple,
about Mom and Sam's age, nestled in beach
chairs, reading under a striped umbrella.

The woman looks up from her book and
smiles at us.

Suddenly it strikes me. JFK and I aren't talking. We're just walking together, enjoying each
other's company. And it doesn't seem strange
at all.

'My father said you wrote a great letter about that organization trying to build houses for poor people,' JFK says.

'Come Home Cape Cod,' I say.

'My dad's giving it prime placement on Sunday's editorial page, setting it off in its own special box so it will really stand out.'

'Tell him I said thank you. I hope it does some good.'

We walk further and further along the Spit.

There's a man in a red kayak, two sunfish sailboats, a fishing rig far off shore.

'I'm sorry nobody was up for another big service project,' JFK says. 'Maybe next year.'

'That's OK. I understand.'

'But the book drive is a good idea. You've probably got enough books of your own to stock three or four school libraries.' He smiles at me and we laugh.

'You too,' I say. 'Didn't you write on Tina's matchmaking survey that you couldn't pick just one favourite book because there were too many . . .'

And as soon as I bring up that stupid survey

I regret it. I picture Mariel Sanchez. And what was she doing at the dance anyway? And where did she get the gown and . . .

'Willa?'

'What?'

'Where are you?' JFK is staring at me.

'Oh, sorry.' I laugh and he laughs too.

We walk all the way out to the tip of the Spit. The wind picks up and whips my hair back. We turn the corner and there it is.

Our spot. Like our own private island. No one else is around. Good.

'Do you want to eat now?' JFK says, setting the bag down. 'I'm hungry.'

'Sure.' I lay out the blanket, smooth down the corners. I take out the food, set out our plates. JFK opens cans of soda.

He bites into the chicken and chews. 'This is great. Thanks.'

'You're welcome, but I can't take credit for it. Rosie made it. Tuna fish is about the extent of my culinary talents.'

'Tuna fish is good,' JFK says, 'nothing wrong with tuna fish.'

A seagull lands a short distance away and hurry-stops-hurry-stops towards us, trying to figure out if we're going to share. 'Get out of here,' JFK says, laughing. He throws a piece of roll down the beach to shoo the bird away. I stare at his long, tanned arm, the yellow band on his wrist, 'live strong'.

'Have you written any new lyrics,' I ask. JFK writes rap music. He shared some of his rhymes with me. They're good. He says rap is 'like poetry except it's music'.

'Not really.' He takes more chicken. 'I'm pretty tied up with baseball.'

'Have you ever done any acting?' I ask. 'You know, a theatre production?'

JFK laughs. 'Where did that come from?' He wipes barbecue sauce off of his chin. 'All right, listen. Don't tell Jessie and Luke or anybody, but when we lived in Minnesota, I did *Romeo and Juliet*.'

'Really? That's great. What part did you play?'

'Believe it or not, Romeo.'

Believe it? Of course I can believe it. Oh how I would love to have been Juliet.

'Why?' he asks.

'I have a motive.'

JFK smiles. 'What's that?'

'Do you know the play *Our Town*?'

He doesn't, so I tell him all about it, especially about George Gibbs and Emily Webb. 'It's supposed to be the greatest American play of all time. Auditions are next week and I'm trying out and I was hoping maybe you would too.'

'Sure.'

'Really?' That was easy.

'Sure, why not. And it will get my mom off my back. She's disappointed that I gave up piano lessons. Since I was little, she always made me do something in the arts to balance out all the sports, and I guess this counts for culture, right?'

'Oh, absolutely. Definitely culture. And Nana's got copies of the play in the store.'

'Great, I'll buy one tomorrow,' he says.

My heart is pounding. *This is perfect*.

'Willa?'

'What?'

He looks over his shoulders, up and down the beach. 'So if I get the part of George and you're Emily and we get married, do we kiss at the wedding?'

'That's what the script says.'

'Good, we better practise.'

Then he kisses me and I'm so happy I fly away with the butterflies.

It's getting dark when we pack up the picnic stuff and start heading back.

'There's the first star,' I say, pointing.

'Make a wish,' he says.

So romantic.

11

'Mare'

A star's mighty good company.

— Thornton Wilder, *Our Town*

I dream about a glistening wedding cake. The miniature bride and groom figurines on top are swirling round and round, dancing, dancing. They turn and I see their faces. Me and JFK.

I wake up smiling and reach for my journal to read what I wrote last night. I want to be sure I captured all the magic. Dinner on our own private island, the wind on our faces, how we laughed, talked . . . kissed. Then 'the first star tonight' twinkling above. 'Make a wish,' he said, *so romantic.*

I can't wait to tell Suzanna Jubilee. She and

Chickles, her mother, 'Mama B' as she tells us to call her, are coming this afternoon to talk about wedding plans.

Downstairs in the kitchen, Mom and Sam are having their morning coffee. Mom is drinking decaf now that she's pregnant. She's not showing yet. It's still too early.

'We need a signature cake,' I say.

'What?' Sam says, setting down his cup. He smiles at me.

'The Bramblebriar Inn needs its own special signature wedding cake.'

'Excellent idea,' Mom says. 'One more way to brand ourselves—'

'What?' Sam says.

'To differentiate ourselves,' Mom explains, 'like the things we do to set the Bramblebriar apart from all the dime-a-dozen antiques-and-hydrangea bed-and-breakfast places around here.'

Sam looks at me and rolls his eyes. I smile.

'You know, like the fresh cookies and tea at two and the hors d'oeuvres and drinks at six and the Labyrinth and the Bramble Board—'

'Well, that's not why I started the Bramble Board, but . . . I love my business-minded wife,' Sam says, leaning over to kiss her cheek.

'But what about the cake,' I say.

'It's a spectacular idea,' Mom says.

'Good. Then I'll ask Rosie to start working on a recipe,' I say. 'Sweets are her speciality.'

When we get home from Sunday service at BUC, I finish my homework then begin thinking about our new Community Service Project. Sulamina Mum has a teacher friend in Louisiana. Her school lost all its books in the flood. I find a box to begin loading up. Riley offered to transport all our boxes down South in a rental truck.

I stare at all the books on my shelf, reading the titles, remembering. Finding books I can donate is harder than I imagined. The books in my bedroom library are my favourite, special Willa's Pix books. I can't part with any of these. It would be like giving away friends – Tina or Mum. Well, not that hard, but close.

I carry the box down to the Inn library and start looking. I go from shelf to shelf, pulling out duplicates and dog-eared paperbacks and titles our guests will probably never read. When I finish, the box is full, but something isn't right.

I feel like I'm getting rid of leftovers, not giving a good Thanksgiving meal. I want to send those kids who lost their library really good books, the best books.

Sweet Bramble Books.

'Oh good, Willa,' Nana says when I enter the store. 'I've got new flavours for you to try.'

The store is nearly empty. In a few weeks it will be packed with vacationing tourists looking for beach reads and kids shovelling Swedish Fish and malted milk balls out of the plastic bins. Some Bramble locals have no patience for the tourists. They can be loud and demanding. But I don't mind. I used to be a tourist myself. I remember how it feels to know you only have a week to cram in a summer of fun before you have to head back over the bridge. It can make you crazy trying to cram in all that fun.

Now I'm a wash-ashore. That's what they call people who weren't born on Cape, but move here to live. I like being a wash-ashore. It has such a romantic ring, doesn't it? Except of course when Nana starts ranting about some new 'big money wash-ashore' building another 'McMansion' and destroying another patch of Cape Cod.

'Here,' Nana says, handing me a piece of salt-water taffy.

I undo the wrapper, pop it in and chew. The smooth sweet candy slides across my tongue, sticks to my molars. 'Hmmmm, nice, Nana. Tastes like chocolate and strawberry.'

'Exactly,' she says. 'Chocolate-covered straw-berries. Is it a keeper?'

'It's a keeper, Nana. It's a winner.'

'Good.' She kisses me on the cheek, all excited.

Nana has a long-running friendly battle with Ghelfi's candy store for the title of 'best sweets on the Upper Cape' in *Cape Cod Life* magazine. She took the title away from them and they want it back. Ghelfi's send scouts over to see what new taffy flavours and fudge combinations Nana is dreaming up, and every few months I sneak in to Ghelfi's to do some subtle sleuthing for our side.

When I tell Nana about our book project, she throws her hands up in the air like she's cheering at a Red Sox game. 'Wonderful,' she says. 'I was waiting for the perfect time. And this is it. Come on, it's quiet. I've got something to show you.'

She locks the register and motions for me to follow her to the basement.

I don't remember being down here before. So many doors. Nana opens one, turns on a light. 'Look.'

Books. A closet filled with books; shelves and shelves of books.

'Wow,' I say.

'And that's not all,' Nana says, opening another door.

This closet too is filled with books.

She opens another and then another.

'And they are all children's books,' Nana says excited. '*Good ones.* Gramp was –' her voice catches – 'Gramp was waiting for just the right opportunity to start a library somewhere. In fact, when we were in New York City, just before he died, he was talking with a friend of ours about sending the books to a village in Kenya . . .'

My throat tightens. 'I miss him so much.'

'I know, honey,' Nana whispers in my ear. 'Me too. Give me a hug, shmug.'

We hear the bells jingle on the door upstairs. 'A customer,' Nana says. She takes my face in her hands and stares into my eyes. 'You take the books, Willa, and you carry on Gramp's dream. OK? He'd be so proud of you. *I* am so proud of you.'

I wipe my eyes and follow Nana upstairs.

My heart leaps.

It's JFK.

'Hi, Willa, hello, Mrs Tweed. I came to get *Our Town*.'

After JFK buys the book and Nana gives him a complimentary quarter pound of chocolate pecan fudge, still warm from the pan, and a bag of sour gummy worms for his little brother, Brendan, JFK says he'll walk me home.

I tell him about the basement full of books and how the Blazers are coming later today to plan Suzanna's wedding, and then we turn the corner and nearly bump into . . . Mariel Sanchez.

Her long black ringlets frame her beautiful heart-shaped face. She's wearing a denim skirt and a low-cut white tank top, and a necklace made of beach glass: brown, blue and green. She looks exotic, tropical.

'Joe,' she shouts, hugging my boyfriend, chest to chest, tight.

JFK coughs and pulls away. 'Hi, Mare.'

Mare? He calls her by a nickname?

'How are Nico and Sofia,' JFK asks awkwardly.

The two little kids maybe? How does he know them?

'Fine,' she says. She looks at me. 'I'm Mariel Sanchez.'

'Yes. We met on the beach last week.' I reach for the locket, frame the heart with my thumb and pointer finger to be sure she sees it. 'I was the one calling to you. I thought you had drowned or something.' I look at JFK. I twist the heart back and forth, hoping the silver catches the sun, wanting to be certain she notices.

If she does, she doesn't let on at all.

'Drowned?' Mariel laughs, a lilting sound like a chickadee. 'What would make you think that? I was swimming.' She reaches toward JFK. Takes the book from his hand. '*Our Town*,' she says with a sweet-sad smile. She smiles at him. 'I didn't know you—'

'What time is it,' JFK says, taking the book back, looking at his watch. 'Oh wow, I've got to go. Baseball practice. If I'm late, Coach'll make me do laps.'

'OK, sure,' I say, turning to watch him leave. 'Call me.'

When I turn back round, Mariel is gone.

12

Sixteen Bridesmaids

It seems to me, once in your life . . . you ought to see a country where they don't speak any English and they don't even want to.

– Thornton Wilder, *Our Town*

'*I was swimming.*' Mariel's words scratch like a sand flea in my head as I hurry home. The nerve of her to laugh at me. And the way she smiled at JFK, my boyfriend. *My boyfriend.* And how do they know each other? I need to talk to Tina.

But that will have to wait. The 'Blazer Buick' limousine is in our driveway.

Beep, beep, beep. The back door of the limo flies open before the chauffeur can do his job, nearly knocking the poor guy out cold.

'Willa, honey!' Suzanna Jubilee shrieks, running towards me in a hot-pink minidress. I brace myself for the tackle. We jump up and down, hugging, laughing.

'Congratulations, Suzy. I'm so happy for you!'

'My turn, my turn. Come here, baby,' Mama Blazer says, swooping me up off my feet. 'Gosh, we've missed you,' she adds, planting a big slurpy kiss on my cheek. She sets me down and swooshes back one of her signature feather boas, this one fire-engine red. 'Let me look at you.' She shakes her head from side to side. 'Cute as a button, pretty as a picture.'

'Willa, I have something to ask you,' Suzy-Jube says. 'Something important.'

'Sure, anything.'

Suzy looks at her mother. Her mother smiles and winks. Suzy looks at my mother. My mother smiles and winks.

'Willa,' Suzy says, then pauses, 'will you be my maid of honour?'

'Me?'

'You.' Suzanna clasps her hands together, fingertips touching her lips, eyes squinting like 'I hope you'll say yes'.

I swallow hard. My eyes fill up. I've never

been in a wedding before. And the maid of honour . . . that's very special. 'Are you sure—'

'Sure as sugar,' Suzy says. 'On Saturday June the tenth, Bramble, Cape Cod, United States of *A-mer-i-ca* is going to have a wedding like it's never had before. I'm going to have sixteen bridesmaids. That's Simon's and my lucky number. We met on February the sixteenth and we counted sixteen stars on the night we first kissed and, well, I just couldn't leave any of my best sweet pageant peeps, my chicklets, out of the wedding party, but then I couldn't pick one favourite to be my maid of honour, the rest would get all jealous, and so I thought about who I most wanted to have up there next to me on the stage on the most important day of my life and your cute as a button sweet little face popped right into my mind.'

'Popped right in,' Chickles says, testifying to the truth, criss-crossing her hands over her hefty chest.

'I'd be honoured,' I say.

'Good!' Suzy shrieks and twirls me around. 'Now, aren't you dying to see my man?' She reaches into her pocketbook and hands me a picture. 'Willa Havisham meet Simon Finch.'

'Wow.'

Simon Finch gives new meaning to the word 'hot'. Simon deserves his own new word. Long dark hair, sultry eyes, stubble on his chin like he didn't shave that day, a leather choker with some sort of charm on it, a small hoop earring . . . Who cares if he only has two nickels to tape together . . .

'He's gorgeous, Suzy. You make a stunning couple.'

'Thanks, honey, I know. And he's just the perfect man for me. Isn't he, Mama?'

Chickles bobs her head like there has never been a truer true. 'If Noah came back down again and called folks two by two, Suzy and Simon would be first on the ark.'

I dig my fingernails into my palms so I won't giggle. I look quickly at Mother, but she's remaining nicely composed.

'And speaking of arks,' Chickles continues, 'we've rented out the new Cape Queen for the second reception—'

'The cruise ship?' Stella says. 'But don't you want to have the reception here?'

'Oh yes, Stella. We want the wedding here of course, and the first reception for close family and friends. But we've got so many relatives and employees and business associates and, well, Suzanna has a ton of girlfriends from all her pageants, and Papa B and I thought it might be nice to invite all those young people the Blazer Benevolent Foundation is helping us put through college ever since we read those inspiring words on Willa's Bramble Board last year and started doing all these good things with our money, and, well, this is our one and only baby girl and she's only going to get married once and we can afford to do it, so why not?'

The Blazers are loaded. I mean they are billionaire loaded. And you can't even hold it against them, because they are the kindest, sweetest, most down-to-earth people you'd ever want to meet.

'That sounds wonderful,' my mother says.

'And of course you'll all come on the Queen with us,' Mama B says. 'Right?'

'Well, we'll have to see,' Mom says. 'Summer is a busy time for us—'

'Mom, please,' I say.

'Let me talk to Sam,' she says. 'If there is any way we can, we will. Now, let's talk about the wedding. Come, let's sit on the porch. I'll get us some iced tea.'

We make a circle with our wicker chairs. 'Go ahead, princess,' Mama B says, 'tell Stella and Willa what you have in mind for the wedding.'

'Well . . .' Suzy-Jube says, 'I had a dream.' She closes her eyes and smiles, then opens them. 'And I could see the whole thing picture-perfect. You know that lovely lake you've got back there?'

Mom and I nod yes.

'Well, in my dream, the audience, I mean the guests, were all seated facing the water. And there was a boat out on one side of the lake. I was sitting in it. And a man in a costume started rowing it. You know, like those ganolas they have in Italy. That's where we're going on our honeymoon Italy. Neither of us has been and we don't speak Italian, but who cares about talking on your honeymoon, right?' She giggles. 'Anyway . . .

over on the other side of the lake, at the very same moment, Simon is being rowed out on another ganola, and the two boats meet in the middle and . . .'

I force myself not to look at my mother. I'm remembering her Weddings by Havisham studio and the easels where she'd display the twelve perfect ingredients of her masterpiece weddings, and I'm afraid if our eyes meet she'll start laughing or crying. I get a picture of those 'ganolas' in my head and picture these hunky muscly beach lifeguards rowing her, *row – ee-oo, row, row*. And where will the sixteen bridesmaids be? And I dig my nails in deeper.

'Oh, and . . .' Suzanna continues, 'I want tons of dancing. Tons and tons of dancing. Maybe you can hire that jazzy babe who ran the turkey dance you had in the barn last Thanksgiving . . .'

'Happyfeet Hall?' Stella asks.

'That's right,' Suzanna says. 'Happy feet. Happy feet all night long.'

Stella and I take notes as Suzanna talks. I can tell my mother is exercising every ounce of self-control to just listen, open-minded. What

Suzanna is describing is a far cry from the work-of-art weddings Stella Havisham was known for. But, I've got to hand it to my mother. That steely coat of armour she used to wear seems to be in permanent storage. She actually seems to be enjoying this.

'And I want pony rides and clowns for all my little cousins . . .' Suzanna sails on.

My mother sets down her glass of tea quickly.

'And, wait –' Suzanna gets a new idea – 'what about acrobats? You've got all those lovely tall trees . . .'

Mom goes over the menu choices and I explain how we are working on a Bramblebriar Inn signature wedding cake that will make its grand debut at Suzanna's wedding.

'Yummy-yum-yum-yum,' Mama B says, smacking her lips together like she can taste the frosting already. 'Better make it a big one. Everybody in the family has a supersized sweet tooth. Never skimp on the suga' when the Blazers are in town.'

'The signature cake was Willa's idea,' Mom says. 'I think she has my wedding-planner genes.' She sets her pen on the table and rests her hand on her stomach.

I smile, nodding slightly toward her stomach and then at our guests with an expression like, 'Are you going to tell them?'

Mom smiles and winks at me. 'Oh, and we have some news, ladies,' Mom says. 'It's early and we really aren't telling many people yet, but . . . Sam and I are expecting a baby.'

'A baby!' Mama B shouts.

'A baby!' Suzy-Jube shouts. They rush to hug my mother.

'Wait till Papa B hears you've got a guppy in your tuppy,' Mama B says. 'He can't wait to be a grandaddy. He'll be ordering dollhouses and rocking horses and train sets and . . . is it a boy or a girl?'

'It's still too early. We don't know yet,' Mom says.

'Oh, Willa, how wonderful,' Suzy-Jube says, hugging me again. 'You're going to be a big sister!'

13

Fly, Mama, Fly

Some people aren't made for small-town life.

– Thornton Wilder, *Our Town*

After our wedding-planning session, Suzy-Jube and I have a chance to talk just the two of us. I tell her about Mariel Sanchez and how she and JFK were a perfect match at the dance and how JFK called her 'Mare', when we ran into her outside Nana's store, and how she's beautiful and how she hugged him . . .

'OK, honey, hold it right there,' Suzy says. She stands up and puts her hands on her hips. 'Listen up, because this is important.'

I lean in closer, all ears.

Suzy checks her gorgeous face in the mirror.

Straightens a lock of hair. Turns around and looks at me. 'I always found with boyfriends – and believe me, I've had a gazillion – that the best thing to do is to play your hand straight up. Lay your cards right on the table, no bluffin', and tell the boy you expect the same. And, Willa, don't go getting worry wrinkles over the fish girl—'

'The fish girl?' I laugh.

'What?' Suzy laughs too. 'She sounds awful fishy to me, out swimming when any sensible girl would be home getting her beauty sleep. And . . . we can't jump to conclusions until we know the facts. Only Joey knows the facts. Now, here's what you do. There might not be anything to worry about at all. Don't make it into a soap opera or anything, just say real nonchalantly, "Hey, Joe, how did you know that girl we saw the other day?" Now, listen, here's the key part. Don't look at him while you're talking. Be fixing your lipstick or brushing a crumb off the table or something, so it looks like you're hardly even listening, not concerned at all . . .'

*

I have my chance the next day, when JFK sits with me in the cafeteria. Tina and Ruby are eating lunch outside, trying to catch some colour. 'Spring tan training,' Ruby calls it.

JFK talks about the Red Sox.

They're looking good.

He talks about his own baseball team.

They're looking good too.

I wait until just before the bell rings. I take out my new watermelon lipgloss and pull off the top. 'Hey, Joseph, I was wondering. How do you know that girl we saw the other day –' I put on some gloss and smack my lips – 'outside my grandmother's store?' I put the top back on the tube. I brush a sandwich crumb off the table. Suzy-Jube would be proud.

'Uh . . .' JFK's face reddens. He crumples up his sandwich bag.

Oh no. Not the reaction I was looking for.

'It's sort of awkward,' he says.

Waves rush into my ears, drowning out his voice. 'What do you mean awkward?' I manage to say.

'I don't know if I should tell . . .'

My face flushes. Beads of sweat are forming on my forehead.

'What?' I say. 'Tell me.' *Please don't tell me you used to go out with her . . .*

'OK. We met last year in Hyannis. At a homeless shelter. I think I told you I used to go with my mom to volunteer sometimes. Well, one night when I was there, Mare came in with her baby brother and sister.'

'Nico and Sofia?'

'Yeah, that's right. Mare's father was in the hospital and their landlord was a real jerk. He locked them out of their apartment because the rent was late. Mare was so embarrassed. "We would have paid him back," she said. My mother felt awful for them and sort of took Mare under her wing. She brought them clothes and diapers for the babies, helped Mare's father fill out paperwork for government assistance, even helped them find an apartment here in Bramble . . .'

The bell rings.

'But where's Mariel's mother?' I ask.

'She's an actress,' JFK says. 'She had just landed a big role in some production that was touring the country, when Mr Sanchez got hurt in an accident and Mrs Sanchez had to give up the play and come home. Mare said her mother got really depressed – I mean really depressed. Mare couldn't stand to see her so sad. And so she told her mother to go. Go back to the play, go follow her dreams. Mare said she'd take care of the babies . . .'

JFK shakes his head. 'Can you believe that? Being that brave? I mean Mare was twelve – just a kid – and she said she'd be the mother so her mother could go be happy.'

We walk to history class in silence. I feel an overwhelming sense of doom, like a thick curtain of fog is falling on my sunny little world . . .

Now I wish JFK had said, 'Yeah, we went to the movies once,' or, 'Yeah, we hung out at the mall,' or even, 'Yeah, we used to go out.' That I could deal with.

But no, this is bigger than that. Way bigger than that.

This girl is in his heart.

14

Auditions

We've got a lot of pleasures of a kind here: we like the sun comin' up over the mountain in the morning, and we all notice a good deal about the birds. We pay a lot of attention to them.

– Thornton Wilder, *Our Town*

I wake up the next morning with this queasy feeling inside. What if JFK cares more for Mariel than he is saying? What if they were more than friends? Why did she have to move here to Bramble anyway? Hyannis is a perfectly good town. Why didn't her family stay there?

I pick up *Our Town*. Auditions are tonight. I know Emily's lines by heart. I've practised them on the beach, in front of the mirror, in the shower, and in bed before I fall asleep. JFK says he's been practising too. If all goes well, we'll be Emily and George.

In English, Sam says we'll be studying one of his favourite heroines. 'Miss Janie Crawford in Zora Neale Hurston's groundbreaking novel *Their Eyes Were Watching God*.' Sam holds up the book like he's holding up a trophy. 'This is a classic that should be as familiar to you as *The Wizard of Oz*. I'd like you to read it by Monday and come in with three talking points.'

'Monday' Tina says. 'How many pages is it?'

Sam opens to the back of the book. 'About two hundred.'

'*Two hundred*,' Ruby says, 'you've got to be kidding me.'

'No,' Sam says with a kind smile. 'I'm not.'

'How are we going to find the time to do that,' Luke says.

'Hmmm,' Sam clears his throat. 'Let's see. You'll have the whole weekend. And it takes about an hour to read twenty-five pages. I mean really read, making notes in the margin, keeping track of the characters. So, let's see. Twenty-five pages an hour . . . two-hundred-page book. Eight hours, right?'

People groan.

'Trust me –' Sam looks around at each of us – 'this book will be worth every minute you give it. Every television show you watch this week will fly out of your mind before your alarm rings Monday morning. But a great book like this –' Sam holds up his trophy again – 'a great book like this leaves indelible marks.'

During study hall at the end of the day, I finish algebra and open up to the first page of *Their Eyes Were Watching God.*

'Ships at a distance have every man's wish on board. For some they come in with the tide. For others they sail forever on the horizon, never out of sight, never landing . . . That is the life of men.

Now, women forget all those things they don't want to remember, and remember everything they don't want to forget. The dream is the truth. Then they act and do things accordingly . . .'

I reread these first two paragraphs and underline them. *The dream is the truth.* I circle that phrase and in the margin I write, 'the spirit, the hope'. I think that's what the author means. *The dream is the truth.*

Sam and Mom are busy making hors d'oeuvres for the social hour when I get home from school. Grilled teriyaki chicken with fresh pineapple, on tiny skewers. Spears of fresh asparagus, sliced red pepper, broccoli and chunks of warm crusty dill bread with creamy ranch dip. We serve complimentary appetizers every evening here at Bramblebriar. On the porch in the summer. By the fireplace in the winter.

'I'm too nervous to eat dinner,' I say.

'Have a sandwich at least,' Sam says.

'You don't want to get light-headed on stage,' Mom says.

I make a half a tuna sandwich, grab some chips and some water and head up to my room. I look over Emily's lines again. If the director has us choose a favourite scene to read, I'm going to do the one when Emily gets to return to the living for a day. She has just died giving birth to her second child, leaving behind her beloved husband, George, and four-year-old son. One of the other dead people has counselled her to choose an unimportant day to live again. 'Choose the least important day in your life. It will be important enough.' Emily chooses her twelfth birthday. *That's how old JFK said Mariel Sanchez was when she told her mother to fly away.* I push those thoughts out of my head.

At the beginning of the scene, the Stage Manager, who, Mrs Saperstone was right, is probably the star of the play, agrees to let Emily go back to the world of the living. He says to Emily, 'All right. February the eleventh 1899. A Tuesday. Do you want any special time of day?'

Emily: '*Oh, I want the whole day!*'

I imagine my eyes are closed and, when I open them, there is my town. Bramble. 'There's Main Street!' I cry out with delight. 'Oh, that's the town I knew as a little girl. And, *look*, there's the old white fence that used to be around our house. Oh, I'd forgotten that! Oh, I love it so! Are they inside?'

I can't wait to play Emily. I know what it's like

to love a town, to love your family, to be in love with a boy . . .

Thankfully I don't have to worry about competing with Tina for the role. She decided that *Our Town* wasn't for her after all. She said, 'Well, I love how that Emily girl falls in love and gets married. That's fun. But then she dies! How sad is that? And, I'm sorry, but do you really expect me to believe that dead people can talk? How creepy is that?'

Mom drives me to the theatre hall in Sandwich. She shuts off the engine and looks at me. 'Do you want me to come in, or should I come back later?'

I'm divided down the middle like my one-side-curly, one-side-straight hair. Half of me wants her to come, half of me wants her to go. 'Thanks, Mom, but I think I'll be less nervous alone. Come back at nine, OK?'

'OK.' She touches my cheek. 'Good luck, Willa. I'll be rooting for you.'

Something about the way she says 'I'll be rooting for you' makes me want to cry. There were so many years when I felt like my mother was not on my side, not on my team, not watching my soccer games, not rooting for me . . . I gulp back tears.

I push open the heavy wooden door of the theatre hall. It smells dusty and old. A tall thin woman in black is barking out orders: 'Stage Managers, row 1. Emilys, row 2. Georges, row 3 . . .'

I see JFK in the third row. *Good.* There are about thirty or forty teenagers here for tryouts, but no one else I recognize from Bramble Academy. It's a small theatre, about a hundred seats or so. The crimson walls are bare except for the hurricane lamps. There is a ladder on the stage and three rows of folding chairs. Something catches my eye up above, amidst the jumble of lights and dangling ropes and pulleys. A small brown bird flitting from rope to rope like an acrobat.

The barking woman must be in charge. I walk towards her smiling. She does not smile back. She is dressed in a black turtleneck and black trousers, her white hair smooth in a ponytail. No jewellery, no lipstick, no colour about her of any sort. Except for her eyes: a piercing stormy-sea blue. They land on me like a lighthouse beacon. 'I'm the director,' she says. 'Who are you?'

'Willa.' I laugh nervously. 'Willa Havisham Gracemore.'

The director stares at me for a second and then looks at her clipboard. 'Wrong play,' she says, and turns away.

'*What?*' I am confused. My heart starts pounding.

'No Willa Havishams in *Our Town*.'

'Wait,' I say. 'I'm here to try out for the part of Emily . . .'

Just then I see Mariel Sanchez walking towards us. She moves with the grace of a ballerina, head up, shoulders back, like she doesn't have a worry in the world.

'I'm the director,' the woman in black barks at Mariel. 'Who are you?'

'Emily.' Mariel says, so loudly people turn to look. 'I am Emily Webb.'

'What's that,' the director asks, pointing to a white piece of paper like a label high on the

sleeve of Mariel's shirt. There is something written on it.

'My dream,' Mariel says.

The director and I lean closer to read the
label.

It says '*Emily*'.

15

The Real Emily

The whole world's wrong, that's what's the matter.

– Thornton Wilder, *Our Town*

When that weird woman, who never even told us her name, called up 'those auditioning for the role of Emily', I strutted up on stage first, towns of butterflies in my belly and everything. I gave it my best effort, but, even as I spoke Emily's lines, I couldn't get fully into the part. I kept trying to spot JFK in the audience. I worried about how good Mariel would be . . .

Several other girls tried out after me.

Mariel Sanchez went last.

She walked up the steps and on to the stage

like she owned it. Like she was Emily. Like this was her town.

Mariel Sanchez might have been Mariel Sanchez of the run down Oceanview Inn of Bramble when she walked on to that stage, but when Mariel Sanchez turned and faced the audience, she was Emily Webb of Grover's Corners, New Hampshire, May 1901:

'*Oh, Mama, just look at me a minute as though you really saw me . . . Just for a moment now we're all together. Mama, just for a moment we're happy.*'

And as Mariel spoke I pictured her that night, staring into her own mother's eyes, the way JFK had described the story to me, how she had set her mother free to go and be happy.

Mariel had me in tears. She had the whole theatre in tears. We were mesmerized.

Mariel was Emily. *The real Emily.*

And JFK was the perfect George Gibbs:

'*Listen, Emily. I think that once you've found a person that you're very fond of . . . I mean a person who's fond of you too . . . Emily, if I do improve and make a big change . . . would you be . . . I mean: could you be . . .*'

Yes, yes, yes. My heart shouted. *Yes, I will marry you.*

When the auditions were over, the director announced, 'Well done, people. Thank you for your time. I will save you the agony of a sleepless night by posting the leads right now. Practice starts Monday, promptly at 7 p.m.'

She pinned the list on a bulletin board. I didn't even have to read it.

Mariel was first in line. 'Yes!' she shouted, clasping her hands together. Then she ran to JFK, her face glowing jubilantly. 'Joe, you're George,' she shouted, hugging him tight.

No. I stood there watching. *No.*

It was like the time when I was six and we were at the National Seashore and I was standing in the water daydreaming about something and all of a sudden this gigantic wave knocked me over and my body was hurling – *no, no* – water filling my nose and mouth – *no* – and then my face crashed down against the gravelly sand.

'Willa,' JFK says, pulling himself away from

Mariel to walk towards me. He looks so sweet and handsome and sorry for me.

I can't stand him feeling sorry for me. I turn to leave.

'Willa, wait.'

I run outside and down the block. I sit down on a bench, my head swirling. I look back towards the theatre hoping JFK is right behind me, but he's not.

I sit crying for what feels like hours, and finally I see him coming. I wipe my face quickly and blow my nose. He sits down. 'I'm sorry you didn't get the part, Willa.'

I don't answer him. I picture JFK and Mariel in the wedding scene in *Our Town*. He is watching her walk down the aisle towards him. He looks so happy and handsome in his tuxedo. She looks so happy and gorgeous in her wedding gown. I start to cry again. *Grow up, Willa. You're such a baby.*

'Willa,' JFK puts his arms around me. He speaks in a soft voice. 'It's just a play. There will be others. I didn't realize how much that part meant to you.'

'*I don't want you kissing her!*' I shout with such anger it surprises me.

JFK laughs. 'Whoa. Is that what you're worried about?'

'It's not funny,' I say, standing up.

'Hey,' he says, reaching out for my arm, 'sit down.'

It's dark, but the moon is bright. JFK wipes tears from my cheeks. He puts his hand under my chin and props up my face so he can look straight into my eyes. 'Listen to me,' he says. 'I mean it, listen. When I kiss her it will just be acting. When I kiss *you* it's for real.' Then his sweet warm lips are on mine and I feel like I'm melting, melting.

I look up at the sky. '*The moonlight's so wonderful*,' I say, quoting one of Emily's lines, 'isn't it?'

JFK laughs. 'Yeah, but that director chick's scary, isn't she?'

'Yes,' I say, laughing, starting to feel better. I look at my watch. 'I've got to get back, my mother will be here any minute.'

'Listen,' JFK says. 'Don't hold this against

Mare, OK? She's had a lot of hard stuff in her life. This part, this particular play, is really important to her.'

'Why this play?' I feel my anger rising.

'I didn't know until now,' JFK says, looking away down the street, back towards the theatre. 'She just explained it to me inside. Remember how I told you her mother ran off because she landed some big role in a play?'

'I remember.'

'Well, the play was *Our Town*.'

When my mother pulls up, I get in quickly, close the door and face the window.

'Willa, what's the matter?' Mom asks, all concerned.

'Nothing.'

Sam is up waiting for us all hopeful in the kitchen. Mom shakes her head and puts her fingers to her lips like don't ask.

I walk past guests chatting in the living room, run up to my room, close the door, crash on my bed. *I hate that girl. I hate that girl. Why is she trying to ruin my life? I was supposed to be Emily. I was the perfect Emily.*

I lay in bed playing each scene over and over again in my mind. How great JFK was auditioning for George Gibbs with that goofy baseball cap and glove. How good it felt auditioning for Emily, but even as I was up on that stage trying to be Emily, I kept thinking about JFK and Mariel. I couldn't stop being Willa long enough to be Emily. And then Mariel. How she *was* Emily. The real Emily. And then how it felt so good when JFK hugged and kissed me on the bench in the dark under that perfect moon. And then how awful it felt when he explained why 'Mare' needed this part so badly.

Just before I fall asleep, I picture JFK's face. I could see in his eyes just how deeply connected he is to Mariel, to her situation, to her story . . .

And the tears come like a sea storm. I sob like a baby; like I've already lost him.

I have JFK's picture in a locket, but Mariel 'sea-bright' has his heart.

16

Mother's Day

And this is Mrs Webb's garden.
Just like Mrs Gibbs, only it's got a lot of sunflowers too.

– Thornton Wilder, *Our Town*

It's Mother's Day and Mum is delivering the sermon at BUC. We are in our usual row near the front, me, Mom, Sam and Nana. I'm trying to listen to Mum, but I keep thinking about Mariel Sanchez. She's sitting back in the last row, alone.

JFK and his family are off-Cape this morning, visiting his grandmother in Boston.

'Like the great author Alice Walker explained it,' Mum says, 'in search of our mother's gardens, we find our own. We need to know our mother's story and we need to know our father's story because they made us and we've got their roots and we can't grow strong if we don't know what sort of plant we are.'

I look sideways at my mother's face.

'I'm not saying you have to grow the way they did,' Mum says. 'Each one of us branches out and moves towards the sun in our own new crazy way. But those original roots are deep down there, whether we like them or not. And we have to dig in the muck and pluck them out and study them, see them good, as much as any person can ever truly see another, and then, and only then, can we be free to bloom.'

I start thinking about my mother, Estelle Marie Clancy Havisham Gracemore. Even though we've gotten closer this year, there is still so much I don't know about her past. What was she like when she was fourteen? What did she dream about? Who were her friends? Who was her first boyfriend?

'Now here's your assignment,' Mum says with a chuckle, fanning her face and adjusting the neckline of her rainbow-coloured robes. 'Sure is hot in here.'

The congregation laughs. Mum always ends

her sermons with an assignment. Something she expects us to do between now and next Sunday.

'My mama is long since gone to the angels,' Mum says, 'and I know many of you have lost your mothers too. This is a hard day for us. Yes it is. But if you're lucky enough to still have your mother here in the living, or some good woman who is just like a real mother to you, I want you to look her straight in the eye and say *thank you*.'

I look at my mother. There is a tear rolling down her cheek.

'It might not be all flowers and happy feelings between you,' Mum says, 'but I know if you think about it long enough you can think of at least one important thing to thank her for. Something she taught you or gave you or did for you. Got it?'

'Yes, Mum,' we say.

'Good,' Mum says, 'now let's close our eyes and breathe easy for a minute and thank the other one we need to thank.'

That would be God.

Mum says the only prayer you ever need is just two little words long: *Thank you*.

I hear the heavy door at the back of BUC open and close. I turn around to look.

Mariel Sanchez is gone.

After the service, Sam takes us out to Moonakis for breakfast. We like the owner, Paul. He's originally from Brooklyn, New York City. The food is great and Paul makes every customer feel special, coming around to all the tables shaking hands, paying compliments. Paul says people should be 'aggressively friendly'. I like that. Aggressively friendly.

Soon our table is laden with cheese omelettes, chocolate chip pancakes, sausage and bacon, cinnamon Danish and strawberry short-cake with real whipped cream. We eat until we're stuffed like turkeys.

I give Mom *Gift from the Sea* by Anne Morrow Lindbergh. Sam suggested it.

'Thank you.' She kisses me on the cheek. 'You are such a thoughtful daughter, Willa.'

'You're welcome, Mom.' I get this weird feeling inside. This time next year, my mother will have a new daughter or a son. Soon there will be another child calling my mother 'Mom'. I can't believe it, but I think I'm jealous.

Mom and Sam give Nana a gift certificate to Mahoney's Nursery.

'Thought you'd like to pick out some annuals, Mother,' Mom says to Nana. 'They've got all the geraniums in now. We'll drive you over later if you'd like.'

'That would be great, dear, thanks,' Nana says. She opens my present next.

It's a small garden statue, a cherub reading a book.

Nana makes a squeaking sound. Her lips tighten. I know she's thinking about Gramp, trying not to cry.

'I'm sorry, Nana. I didn't mean to make you—'

'Don't be sorry, sweetheart. It's perfect.' She wipes away a tear, kisses the cherub on the head and smiles. 'I bet your Gramp's got all the angels reading up there. He's probably starting book-clubs and making God read the classics . . .'

Sam, Mom and I burst out laughing. Nana laughs too. A good hearty laugh that makes us all feel better.

*

When we get back to the Inn, Rosie is finishing up for the day. It hits me how it's Mother's Day for her too and here she is working instead of home with Liliana.

'Take a quiche with you, Rosie,' Mom says, 'and, here, I'll pack up some fruit salad and banana-nut muffins. And anything else you'd like . . .'

Rosie's face tightens. She hangs her apron on the hook, smoothes a wrinkle in the fabric. 'Thank you, Stella, but we're fine.'

I think Rosie is insulted. She is a very proud person. I wish she could have an easier life. I wish she could be a millionaire chef, like that Rachael Ray girl on television. Then she could set her own hours and be home with Liliana more.

Rosie has been working hard on a recipe for the Bramblebriar signature wedding cake. So far I've taste-tested at least five that I thought were winners, but Rosie still says she can do better. She comes in early and stays late trying out various combinations of sweet ingredients. Rosie says she's close, very, very close, and that it's going to be amazing. Who knows, maybe Rosie will create the perfect wedding cake. Make her big break. Get her own TV show. Sell the recipe for a million bucks. Become famous.

It's a gorgeous sunny day, perfect beach weather. I call Tina, but the answering machine is on. Maybe JFK is back. I pack my beach bag and bike to his house.

When I turn the corner on to his street, there are no cars in the driveway, but someone is getting off a bike. The curly black hair is unmistakable: Mariel.

My heart starts pounding. I pull my bike over behind a huge oak tree to watch.

She has a wicker basket in her hand. *Is she bringing him a picnic?*

Mariel walks up on the porch, rings the bell, waits a minute, looks around, rings it again, then sets the basket down in front of the door. She gets on her bike and pedals off.

I wait a few seconds, then I bike up the Kennellys' driveway. *What a nerve she has. Bringing a picnic or treats, probably homemade* cookies or something, to my boyfriend. My boyfriend, I walk up the steps towards the basket. I know it's wrong. I look behind me. No neighbours around. I have no right to snoop, but I can't resist. I need to know my competition.

There is some sort of silky green fabric in the basket with a note on top.

Dear Mrs Kennelly

Thank you for letting me borrow this dress. Sorry I kept hold of it for so long. I have never been to a dance before. That night, I felt like Cinderella. Thank you, also, for buying the ticket. I couldn't have gone otherwise. You are a kind and thoughtful person and I am forever grateful for your generosity.

Love always,
Mare

PS Nico and Sofia are still having fun with the green mask. Peek-a-boo!
PPS Happy Mother's Day.

A rush of conflicting emotions comes over me.

Relief that the basket isn't for JFK. Jealousy that Mariel and Mrs Kennelly are close. Sadness for Mariel on this holiday. How badly she must miss her own mother . . .

I refold the note and carefully lift the dress from the basket. It's beautiful. Underneath, there's a pair of silver sandals and a matching pocketbook. I open the pocketbook. It's empty. I feel badly. This is wrong. I try to refold the dress exactly like it was.

'What are you doing?' someone calls. I swing round.

Mariel is there on her bike, staring at me. 'Get away from that!' she shouts, her face flushed with anger. 'You sneak. You spy. Stay out of my business.'

Then she pedals off fast in a flurry before I can even speak.

17

Drawing in the Sand

Just for a moment now we're all together.
Mama, just for a moment we're happy.
Let's look at one another.

– Thornton Wilder, *Our Town*

I need a walk on the beach.

I bike to the ocean with a swirling head and a heavy heart. The sun is bright, but I can't feel its warmth. I choose the lion side of the Spit.

Gusts of wind whip my hair, make my eyes water. I walk and walk and walk, and the wind, like an invisible eraser, wipes my worries away, away.

Soon I start to feel better.

At the tip of the Spit, the wind picks up power. It roars at me with a force so strong that when I turn around, I can actually lean back against it. On a calm day, I would surely fall, but today the wind supports me like a cub held in its mother's arms.

When I round the corner on to the bay side, I see her.

Mariel is sitting on our special spot. Mine and JFK's.

Jealousy stabs me. *Have they been here together? Did he kiss her here too?*

I stand frozen stiff on the outside, a frenzy of emotion within.

Mariel, on the other hand, is the picture of peacefulness. She sits there hugging her knees to her chest, staring out at the bay. After a while, she gets up and moves to the water's edge. She squats down, scoops up a handful, looks at it.

For a long time she just looks at that little bit of sea in her hand. She touches her hand to her cheek, leaves her palm there for a moment. Then she stands, picks up a piece of driftwood, kneels in the sand and starts to draw. *Probably writing their initials: MS & JFK. In a heart with an arrow through it.* My anger rises. I hate this girl. *Why does she have to be so mysterious and different and beautiful?*

When Mariel's done writing, she flings the stick on to the dune, and walks off up the beach. I wait a moment and then go to see what she wrote.

Thank you, Mama
I love you
Mare

My heart clenches. I run to catch up with her. 'Mariel . . .'

At first she doesn't hear me. 'Mariel . . .'

Finally, she turns around. She stares at me with cold eyes.

'I'm sorry,' I say, nervous and loud. 'I had no right to look in the basket you left at Joseph's house.'

'That's right, you didn't.'

'I was wrong and—'

'It's over now,' Mariel says. 'You worry too much, Willa Havisham.'

How does she know I worry so much? We've barely just met . . .

'I am sorry you did not get the part,' Mariel says. 'But it was my dream.'

My dream. That night at auditions, when the director asked what was on her sleeve, Mariel said, 'My dream.'

'That was brave of you,' I say. 'To walk in there with "Emily" on your sleeve.'

'Not brave,' Mariel says, staring me straight in the eyes. 'Smart.'

'What?'

'People should do that.'

'Do what?'

'Wear their dreams on their sleeves.'

When she says this, I get this flash of light in my head, like this is something important. 'What do you mean?' I say.

'People should wear their dreams on their sleeves. So they won't forget them. And so the others can help.'

'The others?' I look at her confused but intrigued.

Mariel laughs. 'They are all around us. And we need them, Willa Havisham.'

'Why?'

Mariel laughs again. 'To help make our dreams come true, of course.' Then she turns and walks off up the beach.

'Wait,' I say.

'No,' she calls back. 'I am late.'

I start to follow, but she picks up her pace; first a quick walk, then a run.

I let her go. I sit down on the sand. I look out at the water.

Mariel is fascinating. No wonder JFK is intrigued. No wonder he likes her. How can I compete with that? I picture JFK and Mariel together at the Valentine's Dance walking together out on the Spit . . .

I get back on my bike take the route through town. I poke my head in the door at Sweet Bramble Books just in time to hear Nana laughing at a joke with her friend Dottie. Nana is holding her stomach, wiping tears from her eyes.

'Oh, that's a good one, Dot,' Nana says. 'Come on in, Willa.'

'No, Nana. I can't. Just wanted to say "hi"'.

Main Street is busy today. The tables outside Bloomin' Jean's ice cream are full of smiling faces. There's a nicely dressed family coming out of Lauren's restaurant, a happy mother in the centre, basking in the attention of her special holiday.

Sulamina Mum and Riley are sitting on a bench outside BUC. When they see me, they wave. Riley says something to Mum and then heads off down the street.

'Willa,' Mum calls. She seems excited about something, so I put a smile on my face and decide not to talk about Mariel.

'Walk with me a bit, will you,' Mum says.

She unlatches the fence and we enter the garden at the side of Bramble United Community. 'The daffodils are done, but look at those hydrangeas,' Mum says, pointing. 'Pretty soon they'll be competing with your eyes for the prettiest blue in Bramble.' I laugh and Mum does too. 'And then the daisies and dahlias will start dancing and, soon after, the susans and sun-flowers . . .' Mum stops walking and looks at me. 'Willa, honey, I have something to tell you.'

My heart starts pounding. This can't be good.

'God knows this is hard to say, and you may feel really sad at first, but I hope you can find a way to be happy for me . . .'

My ears close like day lilies at dusk. I don't want to hear what I know is coming.

'Riley and I are getting married and –' Mum's voice breaks – 'I am finally going home.'

Mum looks so happy. Somehow I manage to smile. I hug her and tell her how glad I am for her and Riley. Then I say I'm late for dinner. I bike home in a daze.

Mum can't go. I need her. I love her . . .

As soon as I reach the Inn, I go to find my mother. She is laying out on the back terrace on a lounge chair. Her eyes are closed. With her silky black hair and rosy cheeks, she looks like Sleeping Beauty.

I smile, thinking about how she hated all that princess stuff when I was little. She'd roll her eyes at commercials for expensive dolls and make-up kits. She refused to let me help her with the weddings. 'I don't want you to be one of those girls who sits around painting her nails, waiting for Prince Charming to rescue her,' she'd say. 'You are smart and strong, Willa Havisham, and you can take care of yourself.'

I don't feel smart or strong at the moment.

My mother opens her eyes and yawns.

For a few seconds she just stares at me. Then she smiles and beckons. 'Come here, baby.'

And something about the way my mother says 'baby' makes me start to bawl like one. I collapse into the wicker chair with her. I think about JFK and Mariel and Mum.

My mother strokes my hair and whispers, 'It's OK. Whatever it is. We'll work it out.'

And as awful as I feel, I pretend that she is right.

'Thanks, Mom. I love you.'

'I love you too, baby. Love you too.'

18

Three Favours for Mum

I'm celebrating that I've got a friend who tells me all the things that ought to be told me.

— Thornton Wilder, *Our Town*

The whole town of Bramble was very generous with books for our Community Service Project. The gymnasium at Bramble Academy is overflowing with boxes.

The freshman class meets after school to sort the books into categories. I mark the four corners of the room. 'Picture books that way. Early readers, like Dr Seuss and the Frog and Toad books that way. Middle readers, say fourth through eighth grades, in that corner, teenage stuff over there. If you have any questions, ask me or Sam or Mrs Saperstone.'

A well-worn copy of *Make Way for Ducklings* catches my eye. I used to love that book. I think about the baby on the way. How much fun it will be reading to a little one.

'Will the hours we put in count towards next year?' Ruby asks in a huff. 'Because we're already done for this year.'

Sam looks at me and winks. I want to say, 'Ruby, we're never done,' but I just say, 'I'll check into that.'

At dinner, Mom says, 'Let's kick off the summer with a picnic this weekend. Why don't you invite Joseph, Willa, and his family too. I'd like to get to know the Kennelly's better. And Tina, Ruby . . . whoever you want from school. Just tell everyone to bring a salad or dessert to share. We'll handle the grill.'

I remember a previous May picnic. Sam had just moved into town and I invited him over for a barbecue. At first my mother got mad but then she agreed . . .

'I'll set up badminton,' Sam says, 'and croquet, horseshoes, bocce . . .'

'If it's warm enough we could even swim in the pond,' Mom says

'Might be a good time to test out the *ganola* boats,' I say, and we laugh. Mom and I have been working hard on Suzy-Jube's wedding. The menu is set, the flowers, the music . . . an orchestra, DJ and Happyfeet Hall . . . we've got tango to two-step covered, the Blazers' family minister is handling the ceremony and . . . drum roll please . . . the Bramblebriar Signature Wedding Cake will make its grand debut. All I can tell you is that Rosie has created the most mouth-watering, wonderful wedding-cake confection the world has ever known. Oh, and I'll let you in on a surprise. I will be adding twelve secret ingredients to our signature cake.

You'll never guess what they are.

When I call to invite Tina to the picnic, she asks if she can bring Jessie. 'Sure,' I say, 'the more the merrier.'

My fingers fumble as I dial JFK's phone number.

When his mother answers, I have this sudden

urge to hang up the receiver, but I don't. 'Hi, Mrs Kennelly, this is Willa . . . Havisham. Is Joseph there?'

Mrs Kennelly laughs. 'No need to use last names, Willa. I think I should know my son's girlfriend's name by now.'

Girlfriend? Whoopee! I giggle. 'Oh, sorry.'

'Joseph's at baseball practice right now, and then he's got play practice, but I can have him call you when he gets home.'

Our Town. How could I forget?

'Sure, thanks. Actually, I was calling to invite your family to a picnic. Here at the Inn at 3 p.m. on Saturday.'

'That sounds great, thanks. Tell your Mom I'll bring potato salad and brownies.'

The next day after school I stop by Mum's. She is watering a plant in a clay pot on the porch. 'What's that?' I ask.

'A sorry little tomato plant,' Mum says, touching a yellowy-green leaf. 'Oh . . . when Riley and I go home I can't wait to buy a little house of my own with flowers out front and vegetables out back. I'm tired of living in other people's places. All my life I've wanted a piece of earth to call my own. Not much. Just a patch that was mine.'

All this time I thought Mum owned this house. She works so hard, does such important work. It doesn't seem right that she couldn't afford her own house.

'I have three favours to ask you, Willa. So sit a spell if you can.'

'*Three* favours?'

'Yep. Sit there and I'll get us some iced tea. Just brewed it fresh this morning.'

Mum hands me a glass. I take a sip. '*Mmmm*. It's so sweet and fruity. I've never tasted iced tea like this before.'

'That's cos you never spent a summer in the South,' Mum says. 'One way or the other we find a way to put peach into everything.' She laughs and I do too.

'OK,' Mum says. 'Favour number one. Riley and I want to get married at Bramblebriar and we'd like you to plan it.'

'Oh, Mum, of course. I'd be honoured.'

'Good. And speaking of honours. That's favour number two. I'd like you to be my maid of honour.'

My heart quickens, my nose tickles and tears well up in my eyes. 'Oh, Mum.' I reach towards her. Hugging Mum is like hugging a pillow. A big soft lumpy pillow that smells like baby powder. 'I would love to. Thank you for asking me. Have you and Riley set a date yet?'

'Yes we have. Sunday, June the eleventh.'

Oh no. The day after Suzy-Jube's wedding. 'Is that date set in stone?'

'Yes, honey, it is. I always say, when it's time to move on, say your goodbyes and go. No sense loading a bucket full of tears. Riley's already ordered the U-Haul van. We'll be leaving Bramble bright and early on June the twelfth, with my few sorry boxes of belongings and a whole big truck full of the books you collected.'

'But, Mum. Why do you have to go so soon, can't you . . .' I scrunch my lips tight to keep from crying. I try to be brave.

'Willa, honey.' She touches my arm gently. 'Believe me, my heart's breaking too. But I lost this man once before and, God knows, I ain't going to lose him again.'

I sip my peach tea and zip my lips. Grow up, Willa. You want Mum to be happy, don't you? She would want you to be happy. 'Hey, Mum, I almost forgot. We're having a picnic on Saturday and we want you and Riley to come.'

'Wouldn't miss it for the world,' Mum says.

'Good,' I say, getting up to leave. 'Mom said bring a salad or dessert.'

'Tell Stella I'll bring peach pie.'

'Sounds good, Mum. I'll see you later. Oh, wait. You said *three* favours.'

'That's right. OK. Now this may be the hardest.' Mum locks her eyes with mine. 'Remember when you were new in Bramble and you were having troubles with your mother and I knew you had a heart of gold and I tried to be your friend.'

'Sure, Mum, I remember.'

'Good. Cos there's a new girl in town with a mighty good heart who is carrying a heavy sack of sorrow and I think she could use a friend like you.'

I don't even need to hear the name. Mum's talking about Mariel.

19

The Lead

Life's awful funny.

— **Thornton Wilder,** *Our Town*

I'm lying on my bed flipping through *My Antonia*, by Willa Cather. That's right, *Willa*. Isn't that a lovely name? When I was younger my mother insisted on calling me Willafred. That's the name she got from combining my birth father's first and middle names, William and Frederick. Thankfully everyone calls me 'Willa' now. Willa like a willow tree. So much nicer than 'Willafred', don't you think?

    My Antonia was one of the last books Gramp Tweed recommended to me. I can still remember our conversation on that rainy afternoon. We were sitting in the bookstore on the old couch with our feet propped up, drinking our signature lemon tea. He said, 'You have a literary namesake, you know. Willa Cather. One of the bright lights. One of the best.' He looked at me and winked. 'And I suspect that one day students of American Literature will be talking about the "two Willas".

Gramp always said he thought I'd be a writer.

I swallow back tears. I close my eyes. *I love you Gramp. I miss you.*

Then I remember what Nana said at the restaurant on Mother's Day.

So what are you making God read this week, Gramp? I laugh and feel better.

I flip through Chapter One of *My Antonia* to see what I marked the first time I read it. If I own a book, not borrowed from the library, but mine, I always read with a pen in my hand. That way I can circle the parts I like and write notes to myself in the margin, little stars and smiley faces, question marks, how something rings true for me . . .

'*That is happiness; to be dissolved into something complete and great.*'

I circled that line the first time. Now I make stars around it.

'*. . . dissolved into something complete and great.*'

That's how I sometimes feel when I'm reading.

That's how I sometimes feel when I'm writing. Fingers flying across the page, words flowing as fast as a waterfall. It's like in that movie, *Chariots of Fire*, when the man says he feels God when he is running. I understand that. I feel God when I am writing.

'*That is happiness; to be dissolved into something complete and great.*'

Gramp said that quote is inscribed on Willa Cather's gravestone in Jaffrey Center, New Hampshire. I'd like to visit there some day. Jaffrey Center, New Hampshire. Grover's Corners, New Hampshire.

Our Town.

I should have gotten the part of Emily.

*

'Willa,' Sam is knocking on my bedroom door. I open it. He has a strange look on his face. 'There's a woman downstairs who wants to speak with you. I asked her name and all she said was "the director".'

My heart leaps. Yes. Thank you. Talk about answering prayers. Finally that dreary woman came to her senses and realized what an awful mistake she made and that I, of course, am the perfect Emily. I run down the stairs.

The director is sitting by the fireplace. 'Miss Havisham,' she says, coming to shake my hand, her long, lean arm outstretched. She is wearing a black blouse, long black skirt and shawl. 'Thank you for seeing me.'

'Sure.' My heart is racing. 'Can I get you something? Coffee? Water?'

She shakes her head, no. 'I have an offer for you,' she says, 'an invitation.'

My head is pounding. 'Yes?' I say, trying to appear calm, trying not to sound too desperate, but unable to stop the huge smile springing out across my face.

'I realize it is the proverbial eleventh hour,

but I hope you will consider joining our humble troupe in the distinguished role of –' she pauses, probably for the dramatic –

Emily, Emily, 'Yes?'

'Stage Manager.' She says this as if it is the most exciting news in the world.

'*What?*' A pin pops my smiley-face balloon and all the air whooshes out.

'Yes,' the director says, clearly pleased with herself, 'I realize this must come as a shock to you. I actually had cast you in that role in my mind from the start, but you read for the part of Emily. And so I cast my second choice, young Gerald from Cotuit. But, alas, young Gerald has had a medical emergency and cannot fulfil his obligation. I need a Stage Manager. Fast. Someone who can learn the lines in only a few weeks. We open June the twenty-first.'

'But I tried out for Emily,' I say quietly. *Don't cry, Willa, be strong. Don't embarrass yourself in front of this cold, cruel, black-hearted woman.*

The director focuses her lighthouse rays on me. 'You see the world through a poet's eyes, all the colours, all the nuances. Emily is not so introspective. Emily doesn't think so much – she just does.'

I let that sink in a bit. 'But that's the best part. Emily is—'

'You may not realize this, Miss Havisham,' the director interrupts, raising her hand in the air as if to say 'cut', 'but I was watching you carefully the night of auditions. I studied each potential player as she or he entered the theatre hall. What I noticed about you was how you took it all in – the room, the people, the ripped curtain, the overturned coffee cup, the kid picking his nose by the ticket booth, even that tiny sparrow flitting from rope to rope above us – you were awake and aware of it all. That is the role of the Stage Manager in Wilder's town. The Stage Manager is the omniscient, the all-seeing eye. *Our Town*, metaphor for every town, everywhere, every age, begins and ends with the Stage Manager. Only this one character sees the past, present and future. Only this one knows the stories of all the others on the stage and off the stage, how all the threads are connected, how each connects to the web, and how it all so miraculously, so majestically, *makes sense*. I am asking you to play the lead, Miss Havisham. Will you accept?'

The lead? I feel a strange rush of emotion. *Me?*

'What worries you?' the director asks, cocking her head to the side, studying me.

'I don't know if I can—'

'I would not ask, if I was not certain,' the director says. 'I believe you have the mind, more importantly, the heart.'

Then she smiles.

And perhaps because it is the first time I have ever seen the director smile, it is especially moving. All of a sudden I feel confident. 'All right,' I say, 'I accept.'

'Good.' She stands abruptly, turns to leave. 'Rehearsal tomorrow, 7 p.m.'

I bike straight to JFK's house. He answers the door. I tell him my news.

'Awesome,' he says. 'That's great.' He hugs me.

'Come on in,' he says. 'My parents will be back soon.'

He grabs two bottles of water from the fridge and hands me one. We go downstairs. 'Want to play bumper pool,' he says.

I've only played once or twice before, but I'm actually pretty good. JFK seems surprised. He wins. 'How about ping-pong?' he says.

'Sure.'

It's close, but I beat him.

'Whoa,' JFK says. 'Where'd you learn to play like that?'

'Oh, I don't know,' I say, smiling coyly. 'One of my other boyfriends taught me a few tricks. I can't remember who . . .'

'Come here,' he says, laughing, lunging towards me.

I giggle and run. He chases me around the ping-pong table. We're both pretty fast. He tags me and tackles me down on the couch. We crack up laughing. My heart is pounding, all out of breath.

'There better not be any other boyfriends,' he says so sweetly.

He kisses me. He smells so good.

I think ping-pong's my new favourite sport.

Summer on Old Cape Cod

*I declare, you got to speak to George. Seems like some-
thing's come over him lately . . . All he thinks about is
baseball.*

– Thornton Wilder, *Our Town*

Saturday is sunny and warm, perfect for the first
picnic of summer.

Sam is marinating chicken and ribs in his
famous secret-recipe honey-barbecue sauce.
When Sam fires up the grill later today and that
delicious aroma wafts through the air, every
mouth in Bramble will be watering, wishing it
could come to the party.

Unfortunately, JFK and his family aren't coming. A rained-out baseball game got rescheduled
for this afternoon and the field is way out in
Wellfleet.

'You know Cape boys and their baseball,' Mrs Kennelly said when she called.

Well, I didn't, but I do now. Baseball, baseball, baseball. It seems like JFK has a game or a practice or a game and a practice every single day.

Mom and Sam and I head out to the picnic tables.

My friends from school start showing up. Tina and Jessie. Luke and Emily. Alexa and Gus. Ruby and Chris Ruggiero. Finally, JFK is off Ruby's radar screen.

'Volleyball,' Luke shouts, and we head over to the net.

As we're finishing our game, Nana arrives in a loopy straw hat carrying cellophane bags of penny candy for everyone.

'I love you, Nana,' Tina says, giving my grandmother a kiss on the cheek.

'I love you too, sweetie,' Nana says.

Nana is a big, big hit with my friends.

'You're mother looks so happy today,' Tina says. 'She's got that dreamy look. On *Forever Young* they call it the Mommy Glow. It's so "in" to be pregnant right now. No more mousy maternity clothes. It's all about showing off your baby bump.'

'Baby bump?' I say. *Forever Young* is Tina's favorite soap opera. It's one of the many things we don't have in common. It's a wonder we are best friends.

Mrs Saperstone comes next pulling a red wagon behind her. 'I made a batch of gazpacho,' she says, 'I hope that was OK?'

'OK?' Sam says. 'It's wonderful. My favourite. Thank you.'

'And this is for you, Willa,' Mrs Saperstone says, handing me a book. 'You enjoyed *Wuthering Heights* so much, I thought this might strike your fancy.'

'Thanks, Mrs S.'

Rebecca, by Daphne du Maurier. I open the book and read the first line. 'Last night I dreamt I went to Manderley again.' *Nice*. 'First things first' I say when it comes to books. I want that first line to hook me and reel me in. This one does. 'Last night I dreamt I went to Manderley again.' *Nice*.

Sulamina Mum and Riley come, each carrying a pie.

'Sorry we're late,' Mum says. 'Just took these out of the oven.'

'*Mmmm*, smells so good,' my mother says, setting the pies down. 'I may keep one for myself.' She laughs. 'And *congratulations* on your engagement, Sulamina!'

'Thank you,' Mum says. 'And thank you for letting us have the reception here, Stella. Willa said you already have another wedding scheduled the day before.'

'No problem,' my mother says. 'After all you've done for me and Willa. It will be our absolute pleasure.'

Riley gives Mum a big kiss. 'Am I the luckiest man in the world or what?'

'I might have to challenge you on that,' Sam says, putting his arm around my mother's waist. My mother smiles. I think back to that other May picnic, when my mother was so uptight, too afraid yet to let Sam into her life, into our lives . . .

I photograph this moment in my mind. All

the happy faces. My family and our friends laughing, talking, playing croquet and horseshoes . . . the tables heavy with food . . . puffy blue hydrangeas and red rambling roses climbing the fence. It's like some Norman Rockwell painting. 'Summer on Old Cape Cod', I'd call it. What do you think, Norman?

Thank you, my heart prays. *Thank you*.

Sulamina Mum is watching me with a quizzical expression on her face.

'What?' I say.

Mum looks around. 'I was just thinking how nice it is we're all here together on this sunny summer day. Especially you teenagers. Fine young people. All of you.'

Mum stares into my eyes.

I know it's one of those moments when Mum wants me to understand something, but she's in no hurry, she'll wait as long as it takes for me to figure it out myself. 'What?' I say again. My friends are running towards the pond, laughing.

'Come on, Willa,' Tina shouts over, 'let's take a boat out.'

'Be right there.' I turn back to Mum. 'Give me a hint at least.'

'Plenty of food to go around. What's one more friend at the table, right?'

Slowly it dawns on me. *Mariel*. 'Are we talking about favour number three?'

Mum's face lights up with a smile. 'That's my girl,' she says.

Well, at least JFK isn't at the picnic, I think to myself as I bike to Mariel Sanchez's house. The waste treatment plant smells like dead fish decaying on the beach. If it smells this bad at the start of summer, I wonder what it's like in August.

Someone has stuck a row of tiny American flags under the dirty Oceanview Inn sign. The place is eerily quiet. The only sound is the droning of an air conditioner in the window of the 'office'. I think of the beautiful house I live in. How lucky I am. I remember the letter I wrote to the paper about Come Home Cape Cod. I hope they get the money to build lots of houses for people.

As I get closer and pass by rooms, I hear all the television sets, different channels, a baby crying, a man shouting angrily in a language I don't know, every window cranked open in hopes of a breeze.

When I knock on number 6, a man's voice says, 'Come in.' My stomach is flipping like a fish on a hook. Then, even before I can turn the knob, the door opens.

Mariel stares at me with wide eyes. She has a book in her hand.

'I know,' I say, smiling awkwardly. 'You're probably wondering what I'm doing here.'

'Invite your friend in,' Mr Sanchez says, wheeling towards me, nodding. The microwave beeps and he wheels back around to it, opens the door, takes out a plate of food. 'Nico, Sofia,' he says, 'wash your hands.'

I hear giggling and then the twins poke their heads out from underneath the bed. 'BOO!' they shout, thrusting chocolate-coated palms in the air towards me.

'Oooh, you scared me,' I say, playing along.

'I told you no candy before dinner,' Mariel
says.

Nico and Sofia hug Mariel the way little kids
hug their mother when a stranger is near.

'We're having a barbecue at my house,' I say,
'and Sulamina Mum is there and Mrs
Saperstone—'

'Oh, I see,' Mariel says, 'they told you to
invite—'

'No,' I say. 'I came to tell you that I'm going to
be in *Our Town* after all. The Stage Manager. I
thought maybe you could fill me in on what I've
missed at practices.'

'Truly?' Mariel says.

'Truly,' I say. 'Do you have a bike? If we hurry
we'll be just in time for my father's famous bar-
becued chicken.'

'Of course you will go,' Mr Sanchez says. He
smiles, shooing his daughter away. 'Go, Mariel,
go enjoy.'

We bike alongside each other. The rim on the
front tyre of Mariel's bike is green. The rim on
the back is orange.

'Mrs Saperstone told me how you saved the Bramble Library,' she says.

We start talking about books. Mariel loved *Their Eyes Were Watching God* too. Right now she's reading *The Scarlet Letter*, by Nathaniel Hawthorne. I make a mental note to put that on my summer list. Mariel says she and her father plan her lessons in the morning before he leaves for work. Mrs Santiago, the lady at number seven, watches Nico and Sofia when Mariel needs to run errands or go to the library.

'No wonder you swim so early in the morning,' I say. 'It sounds like that's the only time you have to yourself.'

'It is OK,' Mariel says quickly. 'In a family, everybody has to do their part.'

Before I know it we're back at the Inn, walking towards the picnic tables, laughing about the director.

'What's with all the black?' Mariel says.

'*I know*,' I say. 'And what the heck is her name anyway?'

And then Tina and Ruby are standing there, staring at us.

'We wondered where you went, Willa,' Tina says, not smiling.

Ruby is looking down at Mariel's old sneakers.

I introduce Mariel to my friends, painfully aware of how Tina and Ruby are sizing up Mariel's clothing: green shorts, too long for the style this summer, pink T-shirt with chocolate fingerprints on the front.

Mariel follows their gaze. She swipes at the chocolate, making the stains worse. 'I should have changed,' she says.

I feel my face getting hot. I look at Tina and Ruby with their perfect clothes, perfect hair, perfect summer-pink pedicures. 'Come on, Mare, I've got a shirt you can borrow.'

When we walk inside the Inn, Mariel says, 'Your home is beautiful.'

As we head upstairs, I realize Mariel is more my mother's size. I fish a few shirts out of my mother's drawer. Mariel chooses a plain white pocket tee. My mother has a dozen of them. I start to say, 'Don't worry about returning it,' but then I remember how insulted Rosie was on

Mother's Day and I decide Mariel is probably proud too.

In my room, Mariel moves to my bookcase like metal to a magnet. 'Wow,' she says, running her hand along the spines, just the way I would if I had just seen all these books. She tilts her head to read the titles. 'Yes,' she nods, smiling, 'yes,' clearly recognizing some favourites of her own. 'These are all yours?' she says. 'You own them?'

'Yes.'

Mariel looks at me. 'You are lucky.'

I smile and nod. 'I know. Listen, any time you want to borrow—'

'Thank you,' Mariel says, 'but the library serves me fine.'

I think how sad it is that Mariel doesn't own the books she reads. It must be hard for someone who loves books so much not to be able to write notes in the margins, circle lines she loves, draw little smiley faces and stars next to her favourite passages . . .

*

The first picnic of the summer is a smashing success. After dark, we roast marshmallows in the old stone fireplace. 'Look,' Mariel says, pointing, 'a firefly.' Tina squints her eyes at Mariel, not smiling, but my other friends seem to like her OK.

Nana offers to put Mariel's bike in her station wagon and give her a lift home. 'Thank you for inviting me, Willa,' Mariel says. 'I had a wonderful time.'

She's nice, I write in my journal later.

But when I close my eyes to sleep, I picture Mariel hugging JFK. I picture them kissing during the wedding scene of *Our Town* and I am wide awake again.

Why did I invite her to my house? Introduce her to my friends?

What was I thinking of?

21

Cheesecakes

Emily: Do any human beings ever realize life while they live it? – every, every minute?
Stage Manager: The saints and poets maybe – they do some.

– Thornton Wilder, *Our Town*

Sam is leaning against his desk leafing through a well-worn book when we file in to English class. It's June and I feel that old familiar see-saw inside. Worried about finals, excited about vacation, worried about finals, excited about vacation. And this June I've also got two weddings and *Our Town* to think about as well.

I look back at JFK. He winks at me and smiles.

We'll have the whole summer together. Just

the two of us. Well, as soon as baseball is over, that is.

When we're settled at our desks, Sam adjusts his glasses and reads aloud:

A child said, What is the grass? fetching it to me with full hands;
How could I answer the child? . . . I do not know what it is any more than he.
I guess it must be the flag of my disposition, out of hopeful green stuff woven.

My mind wanders, wondering about the little son Sam lost years ago. Did he have Sam's eyes? That Sam smile that melts your heart?

'Walt Whitman's *Leaves of Grass*,' Sam says. 'Every summer I return to Whitman's grass and Thoreau's pond. And each summer I find new treasures.'

Sam flips through *Leaves of Grass*. I know he's looking for some passage he has circled. It was Sam who taught me to always read a book with a pen in my hand.

Sam finds what he's looking for and continues:

I celebrate myself, and sing myself . . .
I loafe and invite my soul,
I lean and loafe at my ease observing a spear of summer grass . . .

I look around the room. All eyes are on Sam. It is impossible to be bored or sleepy or distracted when someone is so passionately sharing his joy.

This is the grass that grows wherever the land is and the water is,
This is the common air that bathes the globe . . .

'Bathes the globe,' Sam repeats. 'And this,' Sam says, leaning forward, 'this takes my breath away . . .'

I believe a leaf of grass is no less than the journey-work of the stars.

*

I write that in my notebook. 'The journey-work of the stars.'

I think of stars as stationary. I know people see them fall, but I have never seen one move. I can't wait to buy *Leaves of Grass* so I can write in it, make it my own.

Sam picks up another book from his desk. There's a frayed string hanging from the spine. Another well-worn, well-loved book. 'My other summer friend,' Sam says.

He is silent for a few seconds. We watch him, waiting.

'Thoreau's *Walden*,' he says, tapping the book's cover like he's applauding it, now gently stroking it like a beloved pet. 'I once thought of following in Thoreau's footsteps, going off and living alone in the woods to search my soul. I was burned out from teaching in an overcrowded school. My wife and son had died in a car crash the year before . . .'

The new girl, Shefali, gasps. She didn't know that about Sam.

'. . . and I was desperate to find some meaning in my life . . .' Sam slides his reading glasses back up the bridge of his nose. He looks so handsome and distinguished. I look around the room. Do you all realize this man is my father?

Sam reads aloud from *Walden*:

*I went to the woods because I wished to live deliber-
ately,
to front only the essential facts of life, and see if I
could not
learn what it had to teach, and not, when I came to
die,
discover that I had not lived.*

'That's depressing,' Tina says.

I turn to her like she's crazy. That's fascinating, I think. I wonder if Sam still wishes he could go off and search his soul, alone. I think of Mariel's mother going off in search of her dream. I think how Mariel would love this class. I look at Tina. She's looking at Ruby. They roll their eyes.

'Don't these writers make you want to start your summer reading today?' Sam says.

There are a few snickers throughout the room. *Yes*, I think, *Yes*.

'In just a few weeks,' Sam says, 'you lucky people will have a whole long glorious summer to lounge on the grass soaking up books.'

'I'll be soaking up the sun,' Ruby says, and people laugh.

'That's right,' Sam says, 'nothing better than reading on the beach.'

Later, as the bell rings and we gather up to go.

'Don't forget. Our final text. *To Kill a Mockingbird*. Next week.'

It's late when I get home from practice. I love being the Stage Manager. Mrs Saperstone was right. It's the best character. I've got some of the greatest lines:

Yes, it's clearing up. There are the stars – doing their old, criss-cross journeys in the sky.

There's that journey theme again. What did Whitman say? 'The journey-work of the stars.' Then Wilder's 'criss-cross journeys in the sky'. I love those lines. Poetry.

I remember the summer we first moved here

to Bramble and I spotted that man next door putting poetry on the little billboard on his front lawn. I called him 'the Poet' before I learned his real name.

His name was Sam, Sam Gracemore.

Soon his name will be 'Dad'.

I can't find Sam in the Inn. 'I think he's outside,' Mom says.

The herb garden smells spicy. Dill, rosemary, thyme. The vegetable garden is thriving too. Sam is proud of his three types of lettuce, four kinds of pepper this year.

It's dark back here, but the moon is bright. Sam is sitting on the stone bench in the centre of the labyrinth. His eyes are closed. He looks peaceful.

Sam only walks the labyrinth early in the morning or late, when the guests have retired for the night. He designed and planted this amazing maze himself. It's a circle within a circle within a circle. The narrow pathway is bordered on both sides by perennial flowers and shrubs. You enter and follow the outer rim, then curve inward, then outward, then inward again, weaving in closer, then further away, then towards the centre, then out to the border, as you make your way to the resting bench in the middle. The bench is the bullseye. I think of it as God's eye. Sam's sacred place.

I stand here staring at this good, good man who is now my father.

My birth father, William Frederick Havisham, was a man of big brash wild ideas. His crazy scheme to whisk my mother off on their honeymoon in a hot-air balloon ended in a tragedy. It took my mother more than a decade to overcome the shock and pain of his death. She was frozen like a statue with grief, too afraid or angry to love again.

Sam is a different sort of man. This labyrinth is his Walden Pond, his wild hot-air balloon. Sam's dream is rooted strong in the earth. He won't float away from us.

I think about running through the labyrinth right now and giving Sam his Father's Day present early. '*Happy Father's Day, Dad.*'

I have practised that moment over and over in my mind.

But, no, I'll wait. I won't spoil the surprise.

Tina calls to talk about Suzanna Jubilee's wedding again.

The Blazers will descend on Bramble Friday for the rehearsal dinner, sixteen bridesmaids and ushers in tow. Tina and Ruby are planning on sneaking in.

'Willa, think about it,' Tina says. 'If those sixteen bridesmaids are beauty-pageant winners, those ushers will be . . . *cheesecakes*.'

'Don't you mean beefcakes,' I say.

'Cheesecakes, beefcakes, wedding cakes. Who the cake cares, Willa. You worry about the words, all I want to do is feast my eyes on sixteen gorgeous hunky guys.'

'But what about Jessie,' I ask. 'Aren't you still going out?'

'What about him?' Tina says. 'You know he's my love muffin. But a girl can still check out the bakery, right? Nothing wrong with looking at the cheesecakes.'

Twelve Secret Ingredients

Most everybody's asleep in Grover's Corners.
There are a few lights on: Shorty Hawkins, down at
the depot, has just watched the Albany train go by . . .

– Thornton Wilder, *Our Town*

It's the night before Suzanna Jubilee's wedding and everyone is asleep. I tiptoe down to the kitchen with a certain faded-white-satin satchel. I'm on a secret mission. It's time to add twelve secret ingredients to the wedding cake. The delectably delicious, melt-in-your-mouth-like-taffy, decadently rich and – as Tina would say – *absolutely-to-die-for* Bramblebriar signature wedding cake that Chef Rosie has so brilliantly concocted.

Mom doesn't know. Nor does Suzanna. Everyone will be surprised.

Life can be boring without surprises, don't you think?

You may know that, when Mom was a wedding planner, I used to add a secret ingredient to her perfect wedding plans. My intentions were good when I sewed a cherry pit into the hems of each Weddings by Havisham bridal gown on the night before each wedding. It was my way of planting a bit of love, a metaphorical seed of good luck for the happy marriage that would hopefully bloom the day after the fancy wedding. But, alas, my little tradition caused a calamity of catastrophic proportions and ruined the most famous wedding my mother ever planned.

I planted my last cherry pit when Mom and Sam got married and we moved here into the Bramblebriar Inn. There's a little cherry tree growing out front to remind me.

I'm older and wiser now. Mom is too. I'm happy she's getting back into the wedding-planning business. And now that she's letting me be her partner, I am not going to do anything to screw this up.

But I do want to add something new, something good.

In the kitchen, I turn on the lights, open the pastry refrigerator and carefully lift out Rosie's masterpiece.

Following my instructions, Rosie left a hollow space, a 'wishing well' as I called it, on the top tier of the cake, so that I could 'add the magic' as Rosie called it.

I open the satchel and shake the twelve silver charms on to the counter. Each charm is wrapped in plastic, with long satin ribbons of different colours attached.

I line the charms up in order.

A book for – B
A rose for – R
An angel for – A
A mirror for – M
A beach dune for – B
A labyrinth for – L
An envelope for – E
A butterfly for – B

A ring for – R
An inkwell for – I
An anchor for – A
A rainbow for – R
BRAMBLEBRIAR.

I actually have Tina to thank for the idea. When she told me to go online and research currently popular wedding trends so I wouldn't plan anything embarrassingly old-fashioned, I came across a new-old wedding custom so charming and romantic I knew immediately that it was perfect for us.

It was easy to find most of the charms. The labyrinth took a bit more time. So appropriate, don't you think? Labyrinths do take time. Mr Wickstrom at the jewellery store came through for me. He's such a nice man. I'm thinking of playing cupid for him and Mrs Saperstone. I think they'd make a good couple.

I lift the crystal bride-and-groom centerpiece from the top of the cake and set it on the counter. I carefully place each of the charms into the wishing well, one at a time, smiling as I think about what each one means to me, then I gently drape the shiny ribbons down over the tiers of the cake like a rainbow waterfall and put the bride and groom back on top.

Tomorrow, at the reception, I will instruct the wedding guests to look under their dinner plates. Twelve pennies have been randomly placed at tables throughout the room. Those who find a penny will get to pull a ribbon from the wishing well before Suzy and Simon cut the cake.

There are many versions of this tradition and the charms usually come with a 'meaning' attached. A clover for luck. A ring and you'll marry soon. But I decided to let each person assign his or her own meaning to the charm. Everyone has different hopes and dreams. I think the charms will have more power, more magic, if people decide what the charms mean to them.

I stand back and smile at the cake.

I hope Suzanna will be pleased.

I hope my mother will be proud.

*

Hurrying back upstairs in the dark, I nearly collide with Papa B Blazer.

'Willa!' He shouts, all flustered and dishevelled. 'You spooked me!'

'I'm sorry, Papa B. Are you all right?'

'Oh, yes, fine as fudge. It's just that I forgot to hang the beads.'

'The what?'

'The rosary beads. Mama B says if you hang rosaries on the line the night before an important occasion then God will sure as shootin' send you sunny weather.'

'That's nice, Papa B. Good luck.'

I'll have to remember to put rosaries out for Mum and Riley too.

Just before I fall asleep, I remember something. I head back downstairs, grab a flashlight and go out to change the Bramble Board.

> Suzanna and Simon,
> On this, your wedding day,
> Every bird sings its sweetest song for you,
> Every star shines its brightest light,

We wish you all the happiness two hearts can hold.
— Your friends forever at the Bramblebriar Inn

As I walk back inside, I see Papa B's beads hanging from my little cherry tree.

Life's awful funny, don't you think?

23

Suzanna Jubilee's Wedding

Perfectly lovely wedding! Loveliest wedding I ever saw.
Oh, I do love a good wedding, don't you?

– Thornton Wilder, *Our Town*

When I look out of my window in the morning, the sky is so blue it doesn't seem real. It's that crayon colour I picked to paint a perfect picture again. No clouds, not even the wispy ones. The sun is casting diamonds across the pond and a sweet breeze, like music, is rustling through the trees and over the leaves of grass.

It's the sort of wedding day every bride dreams of and every bride deserves.

My mother comes to help me get ready. 'The maid of honour deserves special pampering,' she says. My hairdresser, Jo, suggested I curl both sides of my hair today. 'Be curly all over for a change.' Mom gently lifts a lock of my hair and fastens it with a tiny butterfly-shaped clip. She fastens the hook on my gown, a silky chiffon the colour of lemon sherbet, with a poofy skirt that will swirl when I dance.

'Yellow brings out the summer highlights in your hair,' Mom says. 'So pretty.' She checks my face, adds a bit more eyeliner and mascara, and brushes my cheeks with a bronze powder, then touches up my lipstick. 'There,' she says. 'Beautiful.'

She looks into my eyes and smiles, a sweet-sad expression on her face.

'You have your father's eyes. Sparkling like the sea on a sunny summer day.'

My birth father, William Frederick Havisham. I remember she described his eyes that way in a poem I found long ago in a heart-shaped box in her closet.

'Sam has blue eyes too,' I say.

'That's right,' Mom says, her face brightening. She looks at the clock. 'Oh, I need to get dressed myself. It's nearly show time!'

*

The sixteen bridesmaids are gathered downstairs in the living room. Sam is out by the pond overseeing the ushers with the seating of guests. The bride and groom are safely sequestered out in their matching 'ganolas' on either side of the pond, shaded from view until the wedding begins.

The beauty queens are buzzing about in a flurry, checking each other's hair and make-up, adjusting their sashes in the mirror. Suzanna generously said they could all wear their favourite pageant gowns and so no two bridesmaids are dressed alike.

'Suzanna Jubilee is a sugarplum, a sugar-coated sugarplum,' Miss Georgia Grown 2008 gushes, adjusting the tiara nestled in a towering bouffant of tomato-red hair. 'Imagine lettin' us pick our favourite pageant gowns instead of matching us up together like a string of paper dolls.'

'Suzy-Jube isn't threatened by other people's beauty,' Miss Whappinger Falls 2007 says, dabbing some perfume down the valley on her chest. Mom had to kick Sam under the table at the rehearsal dinner to stop him from staring at Miss Whappinger.

The grandfather clock chimes 3 p.m., and Sam pops his head into the room, so handsome in his tuxedo. 'The guests have all been seated.'

'What a stud,' Miss Southern Tier Dairy Queen whispers to Miss Mint Julep. 'Wouldn't toss him off the porch for eating cookies.'

'Shhh,' Miss Julep says, giggling and nodding towards me. 'That's her father.'

We process in to a song by Kenny Rogers. Simon's 'hero', Suzanna explained. Poor Tina and Ruby were so disappointed when they crashed the rehearsal dinner last night. The ushers were not the hunks they had imagined. Simon might be gorgeous, but his friends, most of them roadies for the band, look like they could use an a) wardrobe makeover, b) exercise gym, c) haircut and d) shower, not necessarily in that order. But, when Tina and Ruby caught sight of Simon's little brother, Jace, 'rhymes with face', standing there in his faded jeans, T-shirt and cowboy hat, they started drooling like toddlers in front of the Swedish Fish bin at Nana's candy store.

'He's the *best man*?' Tina said. 'Oh my God, Willa, that means he's *yours*.'

'What?' I said.

'You're the maid of honour, silly. He's the best man. That makes him *yours*!'

When they took Jace's picture for the fourth time, I had to boot Tina and Ruby out the door.

Jace sat with me at the rehearsal dinner. He talked about football and rodeos, neither of which I know the slightest thing about, but I would have been speechless anyway. Jace is eighteen, going to college in the fall. 'We've got an easy job,' he said. 'Sixteen couples to follow walking in. How can we screw that up, right? I hand Simon the rings. You take Suzy's bouquet. I do, I do, we're done, let's party.'

The sixteen bridesmaids process forward and now it's our turn. Jace, rhymes with face, handsome rugged cowboy face, holds out his arm to me and smiles in a way that gives me goosebumps even though it must be eighty degrees. 'Ready?' he says.

'Yes.'

I smell his cologne, feel the strong muscles of his arm as he draws me close beside him and leads us forward. I look up at him and he winks and I think about the slow dance we will do at the reception.

When the sixteen bridesmaids and sixteen ushers, the maid of honour and hunky best man are assembled at the edge of the pond, the two 'ganolas' set forth. They move towards the floating dock and the white boat waiting in the centre. When they arrive at the dock, the bride and groom disembark and join hands.

Simon helps Suzanna into the white boat and together they row towards us.

It is a beautiful, simple gesture, the two of them rowing together. Not what you might have expected from a beauty queen. But then Suzanna is so much more than that.

'Two people in a marriage have to row together,' Suzanna explained to me. 'That's what my mama taught me. That's what my mama's mama taught her. You come from different places. You meet in the centre. And then you row together.'

After the ceremony, the photographer takes countless pictures. The bridal party has a private champagne toast and then, when the guests are all seated at the tables under the lemon-yellow tents, the bandleader begins announcing the bridesmaids and ushers.

'And now, ladies and gentlemen, a special round of applause for the maid of honour, the bride's good friend Miss Willa Havisham Gracemore, escorted by the best man, brother of the groom, Mr Jacey Finch.'

Jace takes my arm and we stroll in to the sound of clapping and whooping calls, and then the bride and groom dance their first dance, Elvis Presley's 'Unchained Melody', and finally the bridal party joins them.

Jace smiles at me and winks. He has the longest eyelashes I have ever seen. He wraps me like a hug in his arms. My cheek rests on the slope of his chest. My heart is drumming and my head is spinning. I am slow-dancing with a beautiful cowboy. He is a great dancer. We move in perfect rhythm, no awkwardness at all. The sweet smell of his boutonnière mingles with the wilder scent of his cologne and I feel like I am floating. The bandleader invites the rest of the guests to join in the dance. *Good, keep the music going.* My heart is pounding and my head is spinning. Jace leans his face down, rests his cheek in my hair. 'Nice,' he says. I close my eyes.

When I open them, I see JFK.

He's standing there by the edge of the tent, staring at me. Then he turns quickly, nearly knocking a lady over as he leaves.

'Joseph, wait.' I head towards him, my heart pounding. I look for him. I search for him everywhere, but it's crowded, and then Suzy-Jube is hugging me, gushing with happiness. 'Everything is perfect,' she says. 'Just the way I dreamed.' And then I get swept up in the excitement of the wedding. I'll call JFK tomorrow.

Everything was perfect, the food, the music . . . and the cake – the Bramblebriar signature wedding cake, was the hit of the party. 'It's delicious, just delicious,' people gushed. Some asked for seconds. Mama Blazer had thirds. In fact, so many guests raved about the cake that Mom sent a waitress into the kitchen to get Rosie.

She came out shyly, wiping her hands on her apron. I motioned for her to come up on stage. I took the microphone from the MC. 'Ladies and Gentlemen, I'd like to introduce my friend Ms Rosalita Torres, the finest baker in Bramble.'

People clapped and Rosie nodded her head, pleased but modest.

And then all of a sudden Mama Blazer came rushing up like a cyclone, a bit tipsy from all the champagne I think, and hugged Rosie so hard she nearly knocked her over, golden boa feathers flying everywhere. 'Rosie, sugar,' Mama B gushed. 'You've got talent, honey. That's the best cake I've ever tasted, and believe me I know cakes. Give me your phone number, honey. Papa B and I are going to make you famous!'

24

Two Stars Crossing

*Don't know when I've seen such a lovely wedding. But
I always cry.*
*Don't know why it is, but I always cry. I just like to see
young people happy, don't you? Oh, I think it's lovely.*

— **Thornton Wilder**, *Our Town*

'Thank you, thank you, thank you,' Suzanna
says, hugging me, then Mom, than me again as
the last of the guests head off to bed. 'Thank you,
Stella, thank you, Willa. It was all that I dreamed
of and more. And I *loved* the wishing well full of
charms, Willa, and the dancing . . .' she leans
down to unstrap a glittery sandal – 'my feet still
think they're dancing . . .'

Miss Happyfeet Hall from Truro excelled herself again. She had Mama and Papa B leading a
tango-conga line and then she choreographed

the sixteen bridesmaids in a 'clam cakes number', a sort of high-stepping, leg-flashing Cape Cod version of the Rockettes, that had every guy in the place going wild.

The Bramblebriar signature wedding cake and the silver charms were the talk of the evening. 'The wishing well was your idea?' Mom said. 'How creative.'

But even though it should have been one of the happiest nights of my life, I kept seeing JFK's face in my mind. Then one of the bridesmaids would pull me back on to the dance floor and Jace would swing me in his arms and I'd start having a good time again, but then a minute later my stomach would clench, remembering JFK.

I just need to talk to him, to explain that the maid of honour and best man are *required* to dance together. It's just a custom, that's all. It's way too late to call his house. Maybe I'll write him a letter, bike over and tape it to his front door first thing in the morning so he'll get it when he wakes up.

*

Dear Joseph,

Why did you run off from the wedding so quickly? I was just dancing, that's all. He was the best man and I was the maid of honour. We had to dance together. It's a wedding tradition. Please don't be mad. I'll see you at Mum's wedding, OK?

Willa

I change into pyjamas, snuggle into bed, but I cannot fall asleep. So many thoughts swirling inside. Why did JFK have to storm off? Couldn't he have at least stayed for a minute so we could talk? But I was dancing sort of close to Jace. I can see why JFK would be upset. How I would feel if I saw him dancing with Mariel . . .

I pull on a sweatshirt and head to Sam's office. I climb up the narrow flight of stairs, push open the door and step out on to the widow's walk.

Ahhhh . . . the cool fresh air hits my face. The sky is jet black and speckled with stars. Bramble stars. I close my eyes, breathe in and out, feel the soft cool breeze on my cheeks. I take a deep breath and let it go. It is so quiet and peaceful up here.

When I open my eyes I see a *flash* in the sky, one star burning brighter than the rest. Then all of a sudden, the star bursts and shoots downwards. And then *another flash*, a second star glowing brighter, brighter and then it too begins to fall. I've never seen a shooting star before, now twice in one . . . The trail of the second star crosses the path of the first. They make an 'x' in the sky.

I start to cry. It's so beautiful.

A sign, but what does it mean?

I'm wide awake now, so I head down to the kitchen to put the twelve charms in Mum and Riley's wedding cake. It's only my second wedding, but I have a feeling this will become one of our Bramblebriar traditions.

People had such fun with the charms at Suzanna's wedding, saying how something might be a good sign of this or that.

I know Mum will like the idea. She's forever saying signs are all around us. Beautiful surprises at every turn – if we look for them with an open heart.

Back in bed I lay awake thinking about today,

the look on JFK's face, was he angry or jealous? I can't wait to drop off the note and talk to him tomorrow.

We invited everyone from Bramble United Community to join us here at the Inn tomorrow after Mum and Riley's wedding. The Blazers will have left by then to set sail on the Cape Queen. Unfortunately we're just too busy to join them.

Mum told me she just wanted a simple brunch, but I knew she was concerned about costs. Mom and Sam and I decided that the reception would be our treat.

Mum will be so surprised. I can't believe she's getting married tomorrow. I can't believe she's leaving Bramble . . .

I start to cry again. This time for a different reason. Why is everything so complicated all of a sudden? Just this spring life was so perfect and now this summer it's all crazy. I hug my fluffy old one-eared koala bear soft against my cheek.

Just before I fall asleep, I see the two stars kissing on the clear black slate of my mind. 'X' marks the spot. A sign . . .

But is it good or bad?

25

Mum's Wedding Present

Now there are some things we all know, but we don't take 'm out
And look at 'm very often. We all know that something is eternal.
And it ain't houses and it ain't names, and it ain't earth, and it ain't even the stars . . . everybody knows in their bones that something is eternal, and that something has to do with human beings. All the greatest people ever lived have been telling us that for five thousand years and yet you'd be surprised how people are always losing hold of it. There's something way down deep that's eternal about every human being.

– Thornton Wilder, *Our Town*

I wake up to the smell of coffee and the sound of rain rapping on the roof.

I forgot to hang the rosaries.

I look at the clock and leap out of bed. Mum's wedding is in two hours.

There's a knock on my door. 'Come in, come in,' I shout, moving around, still half asleep, trying to decide whether to shower first or go down and eat breakfast first or . . .

Rosie is holding a wooden tray. 'Thought this would save you some time,' she says. Warm blueberry muffins, juice and coffee. She smiles and shakes her head. 'I don't know how you're doing it all, Willa. Two weddings back to back and the maid of honour at both.'

I take the tray and set it on my bed. 'You are so sweet, Rosie, thank you.' I give her a hug. 'Are you managing the kitchen alone this morning?'

'No,' Rosie says. 'Daryl and Maggie are here.'

Your cake was a such a hit yesterday, Rosie. You'll have to tell me the recipe.'

'I don't know about that,' Rosie says with a smile. 'Your friend Mrs Blazer said to keep it a secret. A tip-top secret. Don't even write it down, she said.

'Oh no.' I see the note I was going to drop off at JFK's.

'What, Willa. What's wrong.'

I tell Rosie what happened last night.

'Give it to me,' Rosie says. 'The others can handle the kitchen. What's his address? I need some fresh air anyway. Your friend Mrs Blazer has my head swimming with all her plans and ideas . . .'

My dress for Mum's wedding is pale pink, a simple but elegant linen. I have blisters from yesterday's high heels. My feet sing 'thank you' when I slip on sandals.

I pick up the silver locket from my dresser. *Should I wear it or not*? And then I think, of course, if ever there was a day to celebrate two halves of a heart locking together as one, today is the day. And JFK will be there. Hopefully he's reading my note right now, realizing how he overreacted.

Every pew in BUC is packed. People are standing all around the perimeter, spilling out into the gathering space and out the front door, in the rain, with umbrellas.

I keep looking for JFK. I don't see him anywhere.

Riley's cousin Birch, the only relative Riley keeps in touch with, took buses all the way from Alabama to be the best man. Birch is older than Riley. He has darker skin, a salt-and-pepper speckled beard. Like Riley, he moves slowly, deliberately, shoulders hunched like they've carried a ton of weight in his lifetime. When Birch laughs, which, like Riley, is quite often, his eyes laugh too.

'Miss Willa,' he says, nodding at me at the back of the church. He crooks his crisp tuxedoed arm upwards and I wrap my hand around it.

As we walk up the centre aisle of BUC, this place I love so much, tears begin to well in my eyes. I am so happy for Mum and so very sad that she's leaving.

When Birch and I reach the front, we part and take our respective positions. The music stops and everyone stands. Up in the choir loft, Mrs Bellimo, in a stunning red hat with real roses around the brim, starts to play the organ. I know all the songs at BUC, we do a lot of singing every

Sunday, but this is a melody I've never heard before. It has a soulful sound, like humming, rising up from someplace deep.

Mum and Riley process up the aisle together. Mum in the beautiful white satin-and-lace-trimmed gown we shopped for in Mashpee together. Riley in a white tuxedo with a rainbow-coloured cummerbund and matching rainbow tie. I smile, knowing he chose them to match Mum's multicoloured minister's robe.

But today Mum isn't a minister. Today Mum is a bride. Today she's wearing a wedding dress, marrying the love of her life.

I scan the aisles for JFK. I don't see him anywhere.

When the ceremony is over and Mrs Bellimo booms out the wedding march, there is not a dry eye in the place as Mum and Riley process out, smiling and glowing and laughing and waving, the happiest day of their lives.

Birch and I join the bride and groom for some photographs and then we go back to the others. Mom hands me one of the tiny vials filled with birdseed we planned to shower the lovebirds with.

Finally the rain has stopped and the sun is showing who's boss again.

Mum and Riley stand in the doorway and a swell of cheering rises up. '*Congratulations!*' we shout, and toss the seeds, clapping, whistling, cameras flashing, all eyes on the happy couple.

Riley looks past us, his chin tilted up towards the sky. He smiles and points to something. 'See that, Sully. God sent you a present.'

We all turn to look.

A rainbow painted perfectly on that shimmering blue sky.

26

I've Lost Him

Emily: If you love me, help me. All I want is someone to love me.
George: I will, Emily.

– Thornton Wilder, *Our Town*

JFK never came to Riley and Mum's wedding.

I checked with Rosie and she said she handed him the note herself.

'He probably had a game today, Willa,' my mother says.

'That's right,' Sam says. 'It must be getting near play-offs.'

Surely he'll come to Mum and Riley's surprise party at the Inn. He promised he'd come when I told him about it. Everyone is here. So many people love Mum.

Mum laughs when she sees the bride and groom figures on the top of her wedding cake. 'Who's that skinny girl,' she says.

Lots of my friends from school are here. Alexa and Gus, Tina and Jessie, Ruby and Chris, Luke, Shefali, Trish and Caroline.

Mum and Riley have a blast dancing with us. They could teach Miss Happyfeet Hall some steps.

Tina keeps looking at me with a strange look on her face. Through the toasts and testimonials and the 'R-E-S-P-E-C-T Aretha Franklin girls-only dance' with Mum and Mom, Nana, Mrs Bellimo, Mrs Saperstone, Mrs Sivler, Mrs Belle . . . and all the ladies of Bramble, I could tell Tina had something important to tell me. It's one of those things best friends know. We pick it up like radar.

'Tina, what's the matter?'

'Nothing,' she says.

I try again later. 'I know you want to tell me something, Tina, come on . . . *what*?'

'Nothing,' she says.

I know she's lying. Now she's got me worried.

Finally, when Mum and Riley say goodbye and the last guests are leaving, Tina grabs my arm and says, 'OK, I can tell you now. I didn't want to say anything before because I didn't want to spoil—'

When she says the word 'spoil' I know it's something about JFK. Something bad. 'What, Tina, just say it.'

'Are you sure you want to know?'

'Yes. What?'

'OK, well, Jessie and I were out on a date last night.'

Last night. Suzanna and Simon's wedding reception.

'We were walking on the beach and I happened to look up at the ledge by Clover Lane, and I saw this couple . . . sitting together . . . real close.' Tina stares at me.

My stomach clenches.

'I'm pretty sure they were kissing,' Tina says. 'And then, just as we passed by, the boy's head turned and . . . I'm so sorry, honey –' Tina's face scrunches up all sad – 'but it was Joey . . . and the girl . . . the girl was Mariel Sanchez.'

'*No*,' I say, slumping on to a chair. I feel dizzy like I might faint

'It's all my fault, Tina. Joseph saw me slow-dancing with Jacey Finch at the—'

'*Your fault?*' Tina jumps to my defence. 'No way is it your fault, Willa. You didn't do anything wrong. *She's* the one. Where does that little witch live anyway? I'll teach her to steal my best friend's boy . . .'

Tina means well, but she's just making things worse. As soon as she leaves, I run upstairs, lock my door and sob into my pillow so Mom and Sam won't hear.

I've lost him, I've lost him, I've lost him.

27

Just Follow the Sunny Road

The morning star always gets wonderful bright the minute before it has to go – doesn't it?

– Thornton Wilder, *Our Town*

When I wake up very early next morning, my eyes are red and swollen. I have no appetite for breakfast. 'Are you ready to go?' Sam asks in a gentle voice. He doesn't press me for details.

We stop at Delilah's florist to pick up my special order.

'Good thing your dad's here to help carry these,' Delilah says. 'Six dozen you said, Willa, right?'

'Mum will love these,' Sam says.

We meet Riley and the rental truck at the school gym. I oversee the loading of the books. The boxes and boxes of Bramble books. There is a reporter and a photographer from the *Cape Cod Times* to cover the story. The books fill the entire truck.

'Good thing my new bride travels light,' Riley says, laughing.

Sam and I follow Riley to Mum's place. Soon a new minister will be moving in.

I remember Mum's face lighting up when she talked about finally having a house of her own. 'The church administration provides housing, but housing's not the same as a house,' she said.

I have a fleeting thought about Come Home Cape Cod again. Rosie and Liliana could sure use a house. Mariel and her family need one even more, all of them cramped in that depressing old motel room. *What's wrong with you, Willa? Who cares about Mariel? That girl just stole your boyfriend . . .*

When I see Mum sitting there waiting for us on her porch, I fight back an ocean of tears. *Be brave, Willa, be brave.* I picture all the times we sat on those steps talking about anything, everything; laughing over the littlest things, crying over the big stuff.

Inside I'm shouting, *Don't go, Mum, don't go.* Outside, I put on a smiley face.

Riley and Sam load Mum's few bags and boxes into the back of the truck. Sam closes the doors and latches them.

'Those books will be so appreciated,' Mum says. 'I'll ask my friend to send pictures when the new school library is all set up.'

Mum looks so happy, so excited about finally heading South, going home.

'You and your friends did another wonderful thing, Willa,' she says. 'Saving one library, starting another. I'm mighty proud of you, little sister.'

I catch the cry in my throat. I suck the tears like soda through a straw . . . down, down into my chest, and lock them up tight for now.

This is Mum's time. Mum's time to be happy. I won't let her worry about me.

Sam and I tie a string of cans on the bumper. We tape on the 'Just Married' banner Mom helped me make. She wanted to be here this morning too, but she wasn't feeling well. I wondered briefly if it was morning sickness.

'No goodbyes, my Willa-like-a-willow-tree,' Mum says, her big beautiful brown eyes brimming with tears. She wipes her face and laughs. 'All right, that's enough. If all these tears spring loose I'll make a whole new Atlantic right here on Main Street.'

I laugh and then stop. I do my best to smile. I purse my lips together tight, making little squeaking sounds, pushing the sobs back down my throat.

Sam touches my shoulder. 'Don't forget your gift,' he whispers.

Riley starts the engine. Mum pulls the seat belt across her chest.

'These are for you, Mum.' I hand her a bouquet of sunflowers from the car, and then another, and another, and another and another, until the whole front seat is filled with happy sunny yellow faces.

Two other faces look out at me.

Riley smiles and winks at me, then raises his chin and looks straight ahead.

'Oh, Willa –' Mum's voice cracks. She doesn't say anything for a few moments – 'you are the child . . . the daughter I never had.'

Mum looks at me with so much love, like she's making a mental photograph of my face, every surface of her face quivering, moving, like the sea.

'I'll tell you what I'm going to do,' Mum says, sniffing. She hitches herself up higher in the seat, a smile springing out on her face. 'I'm going to toss one of these sunflowers out of the window, every hundred miles or so, in every state we go through. I'm going to plant seeds all the way South, so when you come to visit – soon I hope – you'll know right where to find me, OK honey? Just follow the sunny road.'

'OK, Mum,' I smile my all-time bravest smile.

Then they pull away, waving, horn *beep-beeping*.

Sam puts his arm around me, safe and solid like a harbour.

At the corner, the truck slows down.

Mum tosses out the first flower.

She leans out of the window and waves.

She waves and waves and I wave too, until we can't see each other any more.

Then Sam hugs me and I start to sob. Sam is crying too.

Sulamina Mum was the sun in Bramble.

It won't ever be as bright without her.

28

Father's Day

George: I don't think it's possible to be perfect, Emily.
Emily: Well, my father is, and as far as I can see your
father is.
There's no reason on earth why you shouldn't be, too.

– Thornton Wilder, Our Town

When Sam and I get home, Nana meets us at the
front door. 'Stella needs you upstairs,' she says to
Sam.

I can tell something is very wrong.

'Let's go out on the porch,' Nana says softly to
me. 'I don't think you'll be going to school today.'

She sits on the wicker couch. I sit beside her.
One of the guests, a nice woman, a teacher from
Rochester, New York, walks towards us like she
wants to chat, but then she sees the look on
Nana's face and sets off down the stairs.

'Honey, I'm sorry,' Nana says, reaching out to put her hand over mine. 'I have some sad news. Your mother lost the baby early this morning.'

'Lost the baby'. I always think that is such a stupid thing to say. 'Lost the baby'. Well where did you lose it? The supermarket? The post office? The dentist's surgery? *Where?*

'No,' I say.

'I'm so sorry, Willa. I know it's a shock.'

'No,' I say.

Nana shakes her head sadly. 'The chance of miscarriage is greater when a woman is Stella's age and . . .'

Miss carriage. The carriage is missing. Well where could it be? What a stupid way to explain . . . I feel so angry I want to explode.

'You didn't blame her, did you, Nana?' I stand up, my body shaking. 'You didn't say she should have slowed down or eaten more protein or—'

'Willa!' Nana sounds shocked. Then she reaches up and gently touches my face.

'Oh, Nana, I'm sorry,' I fall back down beside her, crying.

She smooths my hair, rocks me back and forth. 'It's all right, honey. I know, I know . . .'

Sam takes Mom to the hospital for a surgical procedure. When they come home she is groggy and crying.

'Let's just let her sleep,' Sam says.

In the morning, I take her a cup of tea. 'Willa,' she says, propping herself up, smiling bravely, but then she starts crying.

'It's OK, Mom. It's OK.' I hug her and smooth her hair.

At school, Tina is so kind to me. All my friends are. JFK says he's 'sorry', but he doesn't hug me. I can't worry about him right now. My mom, my family needs me.

The next Sunday is Father's Day. Mom still won't get out of bed.

'It was such a blow,' Nana says when she comes to drop off another casserole. Friends and neighbours keep bringing us food. I guess that's what people do when something sad happens. They bring food.

'She was so happy, and then so sad,' Nana says. 'Give her time, honey. There are many hard things to face in this world, but few harder than the loss of a baby.'

And I was going to be a big sister.

Father's Day.

I looked forward to this day for so long. I planned to say that word, 'Dad', to Sam, but now I can't. It would be too sad for him. For three whole months Sam thought he was going to be a new dad, a new father to a sweet tiny baby . . . maybe even a boy . . .

After lunch, I see Sam out working in the garden.

I want to talk to him.

I see Sam heading to the kitchen to start preparing dinner.

I want to talk to him.

It's late and the last guest has finished playing a favourite song on the piano. A breeze is lifting the curtains, better to hear the crickets chirping outside.

Go, Willa, the voice inside me says. *Go, Willa, now.*

Sam is sitting in the library, his head nodding forward into a book.

'Sam?'

He sees me and smiles. 'Willa.'

He isn't annoyed that I've disturbed him, caught him nearly falling asleep.

I walk to his chair. I stare steel-straight into his eyes. Blue to blue.

'Happy Father's Day . . . *Dad*.'

Sam's lips quiver.

'Thank you, Willa. You don't know what a gift—'

'I can't imagine how sad you must be losing the baby,' I say. 'I know how much you and Mom wanted . . . I did too . . . and I know it's not nearly the same—'

'Willa,' he says. He shakes his head. 'It is so hard to lose the baby. But the gift you are giving me –' he sucks in a deep breath and smiles his beautiful, wonderful special Sam smile – 'We chose to have a baby. But *you*, you *chose me* to be your dad. And I am deeply honoured.'

Opening Night

Look, it's clearing up. The stars are coming out.

— Thornton Wilder, *Our Town*

It's June the twenty-first. Opening Night for *Our Town*.

JFK and I finally had a chance to talk after practice the other day. I explained about how I was just dancing with Jace, and JFK said, 'Don't worry about it.'

But I could tell he was still mad. I wanted to confront him about how Tina saw him kissing Mariel on the beach, but I don't want to push him even further away.

'Give him some time to cool off,' Tina said.

'Boys have big egos. Give him some space. He'll come around.'

How much space does he need? I can't stand us not talking to each other.

Every night at practice as I heard him say, 'I love you, Emily,' staring into Mariel's eyes . . . every time I watched them kiss in the wedding scene, I felt my stomach being wrung out like a towel, *twisted, twisted, twisted*, until every last drop dripped out.

The director finally told us her name after our final rehearsal last night.

Abilene Muhlfelder.

'Why didn't you tell us before' I asked.

'Because it was irrelevant,' she said. 'In *Our Town*, I am the director. And you are the Stage Manager. And Mariel is Emily. Our other identities have no place in this theatre hall. No place on this stage.'

Opening Night is sold out. I find a crack in the red velvet curtains and spot them there in the first row. My family. Mom and Dad and Nana.

Tina said she would be here. I'm sure she's out there somewhere. And Mrs Saperstone, and all my friends. I feel Gramp here too. I picture Mum, then force myself to focus. On cue, I walk out on to the stage. I feel the heat of the lights on my face.

I am not Willa. I am the Stage Manager. I take a deep breath and begin:

This play is called Our Town. *It was written by Thornton Wilder; produced and directed by Miss Abilene Muhlfelder . . .*

I finish my first lines and other actors take the stage, and as much as I try to stay 'in character' I can't help thinking, You are JFK, not George; you are Mariel, not Emily.

That night on the beach you said that when you kiss her in the wedding scene, you'll be acting, but when you kiss me, it's for real . . .

And then it's Act Two, the wedding scene, and Emily – Mariel – is processing in on Mr Webb's arm and she meets up with George – JFK – and they come to stand together in front of me. In this scene I play the minister. I have to marry them.

JFK and Mariel have their backs to the audience, facing me. I alone can see their eyes.

The rings are exchanged. He kisses her.

And then, for the briefest moment, JFK tilts his face ever so slightly towards me and, with the eye that only I can see – not Mariel; not the audience – JFK winks at me.

On the outside I retain the composure of the Stage Manager.

Inside, Willa and the entire towns of butterflies are doing a happy dance.

30

A Welcome Wash-Ashore

The town's gettin' bigger every year.

– **Thornton Wilder**, *Our Town*

The curtain closes on Opening Night to thunderous applause. The actors with the smaller roles walk back out on stage first, and then the Gibbs family, the Webb Family, JFK, then Mariel, then me. I hear Mom and Nana shouting, 'Bravo, bravo!' Sam whistling. Tina cheering like she's at a Patriots' game, *'Go, Willa! Go, Willa!'*

Backstage, Mom hands me a bouquet of yellow roses. Sam takes pictures. I see Mariel Sanchez's father, his face brimming with pride, shaking his clenched fists victoriously in the air. Mariel is being interviewed by the arts and entertainment reporter for the *Cape Cod Times*. The photographer checks the spelling of her name for the byline.

Mariel was the perfect Emily. Too bad her mother wasn't there.

I am dying to talk to JFK, but it will have to wait.

Abilene Muhlfelder shakes my hand. 'Well done,' she whispers.

JFK's father, Mr Kennelly, walks towards me with a woman I have never seen before. 'Willa, if you have a minute, I'd like to introduce you to Mrs Emma Barrett.'

The pretty woman, with silver white hair, pale blue grey with specks of amber, maybe Nana's age, extends her hand. 'It is so nice to finally meet you, Willa,' she says.

Behind us, Mariel and her father are leaving. I don't see JFK anywhere.

'I've just moved in to New Seabury,' Mrs Barrett says. 'My husband and I recently retired. We've always wanted to live on Cape Cod. It's been our dream for so many . . .'

I'm trying to focus on this nice lady, but I want to go find JFK, *now*.

'. . . and we've been subscribing to the *Cape Cod Times* –' she continues – 'trying to learn as much as we can, in anticipation of becoming "good wash-ashores" as they say. We know that transplants aren't always welcomed with open arms . . .'

Mr Kennelly laughs. 'You are the most welcome sort of wash-ashore, Emma.'

Mrs Barrett smiles. 'Well, thank you, Stephen. We will certainly try to—'

'Excuse me,' I say, flustered and trapped. 'But I need to go. It was nice meeting you, Mrs Barrett. Welcome to Cape Cod—'

'Wait a second, Willa,' Mr Kennelly says.

'Yes, just one moment, please,' Mrs Barrett says. 'I wanted to tell you, Willa, that my husband and I followed the story of your saving the Bramble Library. That was wonderful. And then more recently we read your editorial letter urging people to help support the work of the new Come Home Cape Cod organization and, well, we thought, good for her. Look at how one girl is making such a difference.'

This is lovely, but I really need to find my boyfriend.

'Life has been good to me and Jonathan. It's time we gave something back . . .'

Good, good, good, but I really need to go . . .

'. . . and so, in celebration of our fiftieth wedding anniversary, we have decided to put a hundred thousand dollars into an endowed trust fund, from which Come Home Cape Cod will be able to draw enough interest to build one new house a year for a deserving Cape Cod family. And I just wanted to thank you personally for inspiring us.'

'*Aaaah*,' I gasp, speechless.

I feel a hand on one shoulder and another on the other. Mom and Dad are behind me, eyes bright with pride. They heard the whole thing.

And so did JFK.

He is standing behind my parents with a smile on his beautiful face. He winks at me and nods towards the door like, *Come on, let's get out of here.*

*

'Are you sure I'm still good enough for you?' JFK says. 'When word gets out about this, television crews will be descending on Bramble, and thousands of guys all over the country will see you on the morning news, see how pretty you are . . .'

Pretty . . . I like that. That's light years better than cute. But what about Mariel?

And so I just blurt it out.

'Tina saw you and Mariel together on the beach the night of Suzanna's wedding.'

'*What?* You mean the night you were dancing all hot and heavy with the cowboy dude?'

'He was the best man, Joseph. It's a tradition. The maid of honour and best man have to dance—'

'Well, you didn't have to enjoy it so much.'

'At least I didn't *kiss* him. Tina saw you kissing Mari—'

'Tina's wrong,' JFK says, angry. 'Tell Tina to mind her own business.'

'Well, what were you doing with Mariel then?'

'I was being a friend,' he says. He stands up, angry, walks away a bit, turns around and says, more calmly, 'Mare was upset that night. I felt really bad for her. She had sent her mother a letter asking her to come home for Opening Night, telling her that she was going to play Emily, just like she had done. Her mother never responded. Mare's letter got returned, no forwarding address. I was just being a friend, Willa. That's all.'

31

A New Day

I always say: happiness, that's the great thing!
The important thing is to be happy.

– Thornton Wilder, *Our Town*

My alarm goes off. I look at the clock. If I hurry, I can make it.

When I get to the beach, there is already someone sitting on the top step of the beach steps by the wild pink rugosa bushes. My spot.

Mariel smiles when she sees me.

'Good morning,' she says.

'Good morning.'

Mariel slides across the step, making room for me.

I sit down.

We stare out at the horizon.

It's the end of June. School's out.

Two whole long glorious months stretching out like forever before me.

Later, I'll take my summer reading list to Sweet Bramble Books, grab a bag of taffy, then pack a lunch, head to the beach, and read all afternoon.

JFK's team is at the state finals. Tina's off on a shopping spree with her mother.

Maybe I'll ask Mariel to join me.

I made a promise to Mum to be nice to her and, besides, I think we could be good friends. We have a lot in common. Maybe even more than Tina and I do.

So much has happened in the three short months since I first saw Mariel standing on the jetty. I was so angry at this mysterious girl for disrupting my perfect little world. My beach. My boyfriend. My library. My town.

Today we sit silently, lost in our thoughts, waiting for the same sun.

A red ribbon tops the orange one now. It is almost time.

Our Town was a good experience, but I don't think acting is my talent. The reviewer said I gave 'a solid if uninspired performance' as the Stage Manager, but that a Bramble newcomer, Miss Mariel Sanchez, was 'brilliant in the role of Emily'. She 'lit up the stage' and 'conveyed an emotional depth truly stunning in one so young'. The headline read 'A Star is Born in Bramble'.

And yet, surprisingly, I am not jealous. Mariel has her gifts and I have mine.

Maybe I'm meant to write the plays and Mariel to perform them.

'Should be soon,' I say.

'Yes.'

We sit, side by side, waiting.

Mariel has as much right to be here as I do.

There is plenty of beach for both of us.

Plenty of boys.

Plenty of books.

Bramble is her town too.

'Here it comes,' she says.

And then, there it is.

I smile at the wonder before me.

I close my eyes and breathe.

A new dawn.

A new day.

Thank you.

WILLA'S PIX 3
(Good books recommended by Willa)

A Gift from the Sea, Anne Morrow Lindbergh
Jane Eyre, Charlotte Brontë
Leaves of Grass, Walt Whitman
My Antonia, Willa Cather
Our Town, Thornton Wilder
Rebecca, Daphne du Maurier
The Scarlet Letter, Nathaniel Hawthorne
Their Eyes Were Watching God, Zora Neale Hurston
To Kill a Mockingbird, Harper Lee
Walden, Henry David Thoreau
The Wonderful Wizard of Oz, L. Frank Baum
Wuthering Heights, Emily Brontë

Acknowledgements

Since my first book, *How Prudence Proovit Proved the Truth about Fairy Tales*, was published in the USA in the summer of 2004, followed that fall by *26 Big Things Small Hands Do*, and the next spring by my first novel, *The Wedding Planner's Daughter*, and, during the writing of the next five books, including *Playing Cupid* and *Star-Crossed Summer*, I have been honoured to visit many schools, libraries, book-stores, reading councils and other organizations where it has been a *joy* to talk about reading and writing.

Each experience has inspired me to dig deeper and I am profoundly grateful for the questions, comments and kindness of countless people: teachers, librarians, booksellers, parents, principals and, most of all, the young people who share their light and wisdom, their energy and enthusiasm like fireflies, like sunflowers, like shooting stars.

Acknowledgements

Also, my very special thanks to . . .

My editor, Alyssa Eisner Henkin, and Courtney Bongiolotti.

My agent, Tracey Adams.

My friend forever in spirit, Mary Beth Moore Barrett.

My mother, Peg Spain Murtagh.

My husband, Tony Paratore.

And most especially, with love always,

my three sons, my *suns*, my stars,

Christopher, Connor, Dylan.

Shine on, shine on, shine on.

Read how Willa's story began in . . .

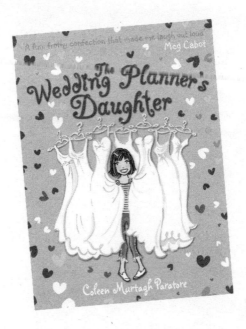

Willa Havisham nearly has it all: a sunny seaside home, a great best friend and her first ever crush. The only thing missing now is a dad . . .

For this Wedding Planner's Daughter, the work is never done. Now she's . . .

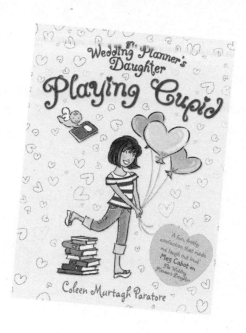

Willa Havisham has always believed in Cupid and the heart-thumping magic of true love. But just when it matters most, it looks like Cupid is about to let her down . . .

OLIVIA KIDNEY

ELLEN POTTER

Olivia Kidney is always moving house. Which means she's seen a lot. In fact, Olivia's pretty sure she's seen it all.

Then she moves into the craziest apartment block ever. From murderous pirates to talking lizards, grumpy old princesses to a boy who smells like a barnyard, Olivia's new neighbours are out of this world. But their extraordinary stories speed her into an incredible adventure. Suddenly Olivia has to start looking at everything, especially her own life, in a whole new, VERY special, way . . .

'Totally hilarious . . . you can't help but love feisty Olivia'
Mizz

Also from Macmillan

The spectacular sequel to Olivia Kidney!

OLIVIA KIDNEY
STOPS FOR NO ONE

ELLEN POTTER

Olivia Kidney is no stranger to strange. In her last apartment building she met a LOT of peculiar people. And not all of them were alive!

Now Olivia is on the move – again. This time to a house flooded by a sparkling lagoon! But floating furniture and snapping turtles are only the beginning. Olivia soon discovers something incredible. Her new house is built on a 'hot spot', where the Normal World and the Spirit World overlap. A place where, sometimes, people get stuck on the wrong side. And when she finds out that someone very special is trapped, Olivia is hurled on the craziest, most thrilling rescue mission ever.

A selected list of titles available from Macmillan Children's Books

The prices shown below are correct at the time of going to press. However, Macmillan Publishers reserves the right to show new retail prices on covers, which may differ from those previously advertised.

COLEEN MURTAGH PARATORE

The Wedding Planner's Daughter	978-0-330-44297-8	£4.99
The Wedding Planner's Daughter: Playing Cupid	978-0-330-44298-5	£4.99

ELLEN POTTER

Olivia Kidney	978-0-330-42079-2	£4.99
Olivia Kidney Stops for No One	978-0-330-42080-8	£4.99
Olivia Kidney Hot on the Trail	978-0-330-44142-1	£4.99

All Pan Macmillan titles can be ordered from our website,
www.panmacmillan.com, or from your local bookshop and
are also available by post from:
Bookpost, PO Box 29, Douglas, Isle of Man IM99 1BQ
Credit cards accepted. For details:
Telephone: 01624 677237
Fax: 01624 670923
Email: bookshop@enterprise.net
www.bookpost.co.uk

Free postage and packing in the United Kingdom